'Got guts, this one,' he said, stepping between them.
'Name's Alfie. You stick close to me, kid. Ain't no shame in bein' small — long as you ain't yella.'

Charlie spat on the cobbles and slouched off, muttering curses.

Job watched him go, heart hammerin', but stood his ground.

'Thanks,' he said to Alfie, wary but grateful.

Alfie shrugged, flashing a lopsided grin.

'First rule out 'ere,' he said, 'is you don't let 'em see you scared. Second rule — find your mates.
Ain't no one survives London streets on their own.'

From that day, Job learned quick — when to stand tall, when to duck, and who to trust — though trust were a rare and precious thing.

See, Job weren't always on 'is own. He used to live with 'is Ma, Pa, and three brothers and sisters in the rooms above Pa's carpentry and undertaker shop. But crikey, Job had had enough of livin' 'round dead 'uns, what with the stink of bodies and coffins everywhere. So one day, he legged it. He wanted more'n just bein' stuck among corpses—he wanted to see the world.

To get by, Job did whatever work he could. Sold newspapers some days, shoutin' 'is throat raw in the smog. Other days, he'd shine boots for toffs what barely looked at 'im. When things were real bad, he'd run with the street lads, pinchin' apples or nickin' a loaf from the bakers—least till the coppers came chasin'.

London weren't just tough—it were dangerous. The peelers were always on the lookout for vagrants, draggin' 'em off to the workhouse, where they'd be worked to the bone for a bowl o' gruel. And the sickness—blimey, it were everywhere. Water from the Thames made folk drop like flies, and the slums were so packed you could barely breathe for the stink.

But now and then, things weren't all bad. Some kind soul might slip 'im a hot roll, or he'd stop to listen to a fella playin' a fiddle in the street. And there were other kids like 'im—scruffy, hungry, but at least they looked out for one another.

Job's luck changed the day he met Mr. Cook, a thames barge captain. Gruff old bloke, but he had an eye for a hard worker. He took Job on as a barge lad, givin' 'im a spot to sleep, food in 'is belly, and a proper job. The work were tough, and the river were no place for weaklings, but Job grabbed 'is chance with both hands.

The barge was moored up in a place called Bradwell-on-Sea, a tiny village by the water, where folk fished and farmed and went about their business. Weren't like London—no big crowds, no factories chokin' up the sky—just sea air, marshes, and folk livin' by the river's tides.

Mr. Cook would load the barge with fish and farm goods and sail 'em up to London, a journey that took the best part of a day if the tide were right. When they weren't sailin' or scrubbin' down the decks, Job'd stay aboard. Sometimes, if he were lucky, Mrs.

Cook'd invite 'im in for a bite to eat. Their house were fair packed— Crikey! Job reckoned it were tight enough, livin' with Ma, Pa, and his three brothers and sisters in the two rooms over the undertaker shop in London. But blimey, the Cook lot—twelve of 'em, and another on the way—crammed into a three-room fisherman's cottage in Bradwell-on-Sea? That's a proper squash, that is!

But still, it weren't the streets. It weren't hunger. It were somethin' close to a home. And for the first time in a long while, Job had somethin' he never thought he'd have again—a chance.

The Cook's eldest daughter, Alice, took a shine to young Job. Though nine years his senior, she was small in stature, no taller than him, and had a warmth about her that made him feel at ease. Each evening, after the household had finished their supper, Job would linger at the kitchen, eager to help with the washing up—not for the sake of the work, but for the quiet moments spent talking with Alice.

Their conversations meandered through all things: the peculiar habits of the household's master and mistress, stories of Alice's childhood, and Job's dreams of adventure beyond the Thames barges. She listened to him as though he were an equal, never dismissing his thoughts as childish fancy. In her company, Job felt seen in a way he never had before.

Blimey, London were a right rough place for a eight year-old lad like Job Symonds.

Streets all mucky, the air thick with smoke, gas lamps barely doin' their job in the fog.

He were only eight, with no roof over 'is 'ead, no ma or pa to look out for 'im.

Just Job, fightin' to keep 'is belly full and 'is toes from freezin' off.

He slept where he could — under bridges, in alleyways, curled up in shop doorways, tryin' to keep the cold out.

Winter nights were the worst, his fingers goin' stiff as old boots, his coat more hole than cloth.

Hunger were always gnawin' at 'im, so he'd scrounge for scraps in the rubbish behind the markets or beg a ha'penny from folk rushin' by.

Some'd flick him a crust o' bread or a farthin', but plenty just turned their noses up or gave 'im a boot up the backside.

One cold morning, as Job sat hunched by a bakery door sniffin' the warm smells he couldn't afford, a shadow fell over him.

'Oi, that's *my* patch, runt,' barked a bigger lad — rough-faced, all elbows and angry eyes.

Job looked up, ready to move, when another voice piped up from across the lane.

'Leave off, Charlie,' said an older boy, maybe twelve or thirteen, lean but sharp-eyed. 'He's just a nipper. Ain't hurtin' no one.'

Charlie sneered.
'Don't care. Ain't enough scraps for the likes o' me, let alone him.'

He gave Job a shove with his foot.

Job scrambled up, fists ballin' even though he were half the size.

'I don't want trouble,' Job said, voice steady.
'But I won't be kicked neither. I'll fight if I have to.'

The older boy laughed — not cruel, but surprised.

The late afternoon sun poured gold across the yard as the shadows stretched long. Angie stepped out onto the verandah, wiping her hands on her apron, and lowered herself into the old cane chair beside Job. The wood of his rocker groaned softly as he shifted.

'You've been quiet a long while,' she said gently, watching him. 'Where's that big mind of yours wandered off to now?'

Job gave a low chuckle, the kind that came from deep in the chest, though his voice was softer now than it had once been.

'London,' he said simply.

'London?' Angie raised an eyebrow. 'After all these years?'

He nodded slowly, eyes still fixed on the line of trees beyond the fenceline. 'Aye. Funny, isn't it? A man can sail across oceans, raise a tribe of children, see wars and weddings, and still... still it's the cold streets of London that sneak up behind him.'

Angie smiled faintly, letting him drift.

'I was eight, maybe nine. Barefoot, hungry, sleeping beneath the market carts in Spitalfields. Cold enough some nights I'd wrap my arms 'round me like I was tryin' to hold my soul in.'

'You never told me it was that bad.'

'I didn't have the words for it, back then,' he said. 'Just knew it was dark, and wet, and that I wanted more than what them alleys had to offer.'

Angie reached across and placed her hand over his. His fingers, calloused and weathered, twitched slightly, then settled.

'I remember watchin' the barges on the Thames,' he went on. 'Muck-covered lads like me haulin' crates for a halfpenny, but those bargemen—they looked like kings. That's when I decided I'd find water deeper than puddles and wind that didn't stink of soot.'

'You did more than find it,' she said softly. 'You lived it.'

'Aye,' he nodded. 'But it started there. With a pair of frozen feet and an empty belly. And somehow it led to this.' He gestured lazily toward the horizon, the dirt path, the river glinting in the distance.

Angie leaned back in her chair, letting the quiet settle again.

'You've come far, Job Symonds,' she said. 'Farther than most.'

He gave her a sideways glance, a half-smile playing on his lips. 'Wouldn't have got this far without you, woman. You steadied the helm when my hands were too worn to steer.'

They sat like that, side by side, in easy silence, while the last of the sun slipped behind the trees. And as the shadows grew longer, Job closed his eyes—not to sleep, but to remember.

As the years passed, their friendship deepened into something unspoken but undeniable. Job, wise beyond his years, came to idolize Alice—not just for her kindness, but for the way she understood him, the way she seemed to brighten even the gloomiest evenings. And Alice, for all her experience, found herself drawn to the boy who was quickly becoming a man, his presence a rare comfort in a dull life of duty and expectation, her Father always on about her becoming an old maid finding a Husband and getting out of their hair.

What had begun as innocent companionship grew into a bond neither of them could quite name, but both knew it would shape them forever.

After seven years working on the Thames barge for Mr. Cook, Job found himself yearning for greater adventure. The river had taught him the rhythms of the tides, the weight of hard labour, and the patience required to navigate its winding course, but it was not enough. The pull of the open sea called to him, promising a life beyond the narrow waterways of home.

At sixteen, eager to test himself against the vast unknown, Job joined the British Royal Navy as an ordinary seaman aboard the *Warspite*.

The next three years shaped him in ways he had never imagined.

He learned the art of sailing on the open ocean — how to reef and furl, how to climb the rigging in a gale without looking down, how to find the shape of the wind just by watching the ripples on the water.

He learned the feel of a ship under his feet — steady and sure, even when the world tipped and rolled around him.

But more than that, he learned the world was wider — and more wonderful — than he had ever dreamed.

The *Warspite* sailed out through the Channel and down the coast of Spain, calling at Cádiz and Lisbon, where Job first tasted oranges fresh from the trees and saw streets paved with marble.

From there they headed for the Mediterranean — a blazing blue world of whitewashed towns, hot dusty markets, and strange spices that clung to the back of his throat.

Job stood on the decks as the *Warspite* entered the great mouth of the Suez Canal — a marvel he'd only heard spoken of in hushed awe.

He watched the desert stretch out endlessly on either side, golden and barren under a searing sun.

The ship threaded its way through the narrow canal, passing sand-choked villages and the occasional camel plodding its lonely way along the banks.

At Port Said, Job clambered ashore with the others, boots slipping on the stone quays, the air alive with shouts in languages he couldn't begin to understand.
He tasted strong black coffee so bitter it made his eyes water, and bartered clumsily for a carved trinket he tucked away in his sea chest.

From there, they crossed the Indian Ocean — long, endless days under a pitiless sun, the sails snapping sharp in the salt wind.

They called at Colombo in Ceylon (Sri Lanka) — a jungle world of bright flowers and heavier heat — and then, swinging south, skirted the Roaring Forties toward Australia.

Job remembered the first time he caught sight of Fremantle's low, sandy shores — the red earth beyond the harbour, the hot, dry smell of the wind.

They only stayed a short time — a few days' liberty ashore to take on water and supplies.

But those few days made a mark on Job's soul as deep as any anchor bite.

He wandered through the dusty streets, wide and full of light.
The people — rough but cheerful — spoke with a free, easy drawl that carried none of London's edge.
And everywhere there was space — endless space — where a man might lose himself and find something better.

He stood one evening atop a low bluff, looking out over the wide sweep of ocean and land, the pink sunset bleeding into the sea, and knew, in his heart, he would come back.

Australia was not just a place on a map anymore.

It was a promise.

The *Warspite* sailed on — to Sydney's glittering harbour, then north to Brisbane, before the long journey home to England.

He saw it all — strange lands, new peoples, wonders that filled his mind to bursting.

Yet through every wave, every distant shore, one thought remained constant —
Alice.

And now, alongside it, a second thought grew —
Australia.

A land of open skies, rough laughter, and second chances.

Every leave brought him back to Bradwell-on-Sea, where he would spend as much time as possible with her.

Their conversations picked up as if no time had passed as he told her of the wonderful places he had seen and how he longed to go to Australia a land of promice and opportunity.

One evening, helping repair nets in the fading light, Alice glanced at him sidelong.

'You'll be gone for good one day, won't you?' she asked, half-smiling, half-sad.

Job paused, tying a knot with slow, careful fingers.

'Maybe,' he said.
'But wherever I end up... you'll always be the first place I think of when I look back.'

Alice said nothing, but her hands stilled on the net, and for a long time they just sat together in the warm, golden dusk.

England was changing, and not for the better. The economy remained depressed, jobs were scarce, and more and more people found themselves living in poverty. Job's father struggled to make ends meet, and whispers of opportunity overseas grew louder. Friends had already left for Australia, lured by letters that spoke of open land, plentiful work, and a fresh start. His sister Elizabeth had married a farmer there, and her letters home were full of promise and encouragement.

Job knew he could not remain in England forever. He had no money for a passage, not even a steerage berth, but he had his skills. He frequented the docks, hoping to find a ship bound for Australia that needed an extra hand. Work was hard to come by; too many sailors, too few jobs.

One evening, nursing a tot of rum in a dockside tavern, he overheard a hushed conversation—talk of the sailing ship *Yeoman*, preparing to leave for Fremantle, Albany, and Sydney. Disease had swept through her crew, leaving the captain desperate for men.

At dawn, without hesitation, Job made his way to the ship, walking straight up the gangplank and into his future. The captain, weary and short-staffed, took one look at him and nodded. Job was in.

As the *Yeoman* prepared to set sail, Job felt
a rush of exhilaration. He was bound for
Australia, a land of opportunity, a chance to
carve out a new life. But even as the ship
slipped from its moorings, his thoughts drifted
to Alice. Would he ever see her again?

Alice had known for years that Job would
not stay. Even as a boy, there had been a
restlessness in him, a hunger for more than
the life laid out before him. She had seen it in
the way he listened to travellers' tales with rapt
attention, the way his eyes always turned towards the horizon, as if he could already see
the life waiting for him beyond it.

When he joined the Navy, Alice had told herself it was for the best. She had watched
him grow from a bright, eager boy into a capable young man, and though she missed
their long conversations in the warmth of the kitchen, she was proud of him. Every time
he returned on leave, taller, stronger, more sure of himself, she could feel the distance
growing between them—not in affection, for that remained as strong as ever, but in
experience. He had seen things she never would, lived through storms at sea, battles with
the elements, nights of exhaustion and triumph aboard great ships. And yet, whenever he
came home, he always found her.

For Alice, life remained steady. The barge still needed crewing, her father still relied
on her to help keep house, and there was little chance for adventure beyond the docks of
Bradford-on-Sea. She had received offers of marriage—nothing grand, but solid,
practical men who worked the river and wanted a wife to keep a home. Yet she had
turned them all down. Whether she admitted it to herself or not, she was waiting.

When Job spoke of leaving for Australia, she had felt her heart sink. She had known
it was coming, had heard the way her father and others spoke of the hardships in
England and the promise of something better across the sea. Still, knowing and accepting
were two different things.

The night before he left, she met him by the docks. The wind carried the scent of salt
and coal smoke, and the water lapped softly against the wooden piers. He was excited—
she could see it in his eyes, the same light that had shone there when he was a boy
dreaming of adventure.

Job stood on the quayside at Gravesend, his sea-bag slung over one shoulder, his heart torn in two. The Yeoman loomed before him, a fine three-masted vessel bound for Australia, her timbers creaking as she tugged against her moorings. The wind carried the briny scent of the Thames, mingled with the sooty breath of the city.

He clenched his fists and turned his gaze to Alice, standing before him, bonneted against the cold, her eyes full of sorrow. 'Job,' she whispered, 'must you go'?

He swallowed hard, the lump in his throat near choking him. 'Aye, Alice.

The world's a vast place, and I mean to see it.

They say Australia's a land of promise, where a man can carve a life from honest toil. I saw it for myself when there on the Warspite

The word is there's work aplenty, and the land itself fair bursts with plenty. I'll not be a barge boy all my life.'

'You'll come back one day, won't you'? she asked, though she knew the answer before he even spoke.

He hesitated, just for a moment. 'If I can.'

Alice clutched at his coat. 'You swear it'?

The ship's bell rang, calling the crew aboard. Job released her and stepped back, his boots heavy on the cobbled quay. With one last look—her golden hair catching the pale morning sun, her eyes wet with unshed tears—he turned and strode up the gangplank, past the mate who bellowed orders, past the deckhands hauling on the rigging. The great sails unfurled, catching the wind, and with a lurch, the Yeoman pulled away from England's shore.

Alice forced a smile. 'Then I'll be here waiting.'

She had watched him walk away, onto the *Yeoman*, towards a world she would probably never know. The sails filled with the wind, and she stood on the pier until the ship was no more than a speck against the horizon.

For the first time in years, Alice felt truly alone.

Job stood at the rail, watching Alice grow smaller, her white handkerchief fluttering in farewell. He had left his heart behind in Gravesend, but his future lay ahead, across the vast and restless sea.

The year was 1887, and the *Yeoman*, a proud three-masted barque, stood at anchor in the bustling port of London. Her destination: Fremantle, Albany, and Sydney—a journey to the great southern land, promising wealth to those willing to endure the perilous voyage. Among the crew stood Able Seaman Job Symonds, a wiry young man of nineteen with calloused hands and the hardened resolve of a sailor who had seen both tempests and tranquil seas.

London lay behind him like a bad dream — all soot and smoke and cruel fists. Ahead, he'd been told, was Australia. A land of second chances, if you were lucky. Or simply a place to disappear if you weren't.

Job had signed on in search of steady pay and to appease his sense of adventure . The sea was in his blood—and here he was, hauling lines and preparing for departure under the watchful eye of Captain Elias Mercer, a man known for his unyielding discipline and sharp blue gaze.

The *Yeoman* carried cargo bound for Australia, clothing and furniture for the wealthy and she would pick up spices and tea and exotic fabrics along the way—then load with wool and timber on the return voyage—but her hold also carried eager passengers, fortune-seekers, and a handful of convicts bound for Van Diemen's Land under government orders. Among them was a young woman, Eleanor Briggs, whose presence aboard was a mystery. Job noticed her more than once as he climbed the rigging, her watchful eyes peering across the rolling grey waters as though searching for something beyond the horizon.

In the convict hold were a small number of prisoners including William who had been transported for a petty crime, he had stone mason and carpentry skills needed badly in the colony.

As the ship slipped down the Thames and out into the Channel, the crew settled into their routines. Job found himself among old hands and green lads alike—Tommy Grayson, a lad barely seventeen with a voice too big for his frame, and Owen McTavish, a grizzled Scot who'd seen too many voyages and drank away the memories of them.

'Mark my words, Symonds,' McTavish grumbled one evening as they coiled rope, 'there's a storm ahead, and it ain't just the weather.'

Job smirked. 'Superstitions, McTavish? Thought ye were made of sterner stuff.'

The old sailor spat into the sea. 'A ship's more than wood and sail, lad. She listens. And she knows when trouble's aboard.'

Job let the words settle as the wind filled the sails, pushing them towards the open sea—and the unknown.

Sand, Spice, and Shadows

The *Yeoman* hugged the coast of Europe for a time before slipping into warmer waters. This voyage would not follow the old route round the Cape—it would pass through the new marvel of the age: the Suez Canal. Opened less than twenty years before, it had changed the world of shipping forever.

Port Said was their first foreign port, and it hit the senses like a thunderclap. The desert met the sea in a strange and stirring harmony. Arab traders called from the docks, selling sweet tea, dates, and bolts of colourful cloth. Camels loped past European officers and Turkish merchants in the alleys beyond the port. Job, wide-eyed, soaked it all in.

Even Eleanor, usually poised and quiet, seemed moved by the place. Job caught her at the rail that night, watching the oil lamps flicker in the dusty haze. 'It's like something out of a dream,' she whispered.

As the ship took on coal and slid into the Canal—a narrow ribbon of ambition carved through sand and empire—Job found himself alongside her more often. It was hot, unbearably so, and tempers on board grew short. But Job was learning—the ropes, the rigging, the rhythm of the sea—and something about the mystery of Eleanor.

In Aden, the ancient port town clung to volcanic cliffs. Job tasted his first mango, bartered with a half-button and a wink. The harbour buzzed with spice, sweat, and coal smoke. Eleanor disappeared ashore for hours. When she returned, her eyes were alight, as if she'd glimpsed some long-lost part of herself.

Then Colombo—a lush, humid paradise. Elephants were visible from the decks, and the air was thick with the scent of cardamom and clove. They had two days ashore. Job wandered the market stalls, marvelling at saris of every colour, and bought a small carved wooden fish. He didn't know why—only that it reminded him of his little sister, long lost to the alleys of Limehouse.

Eleanor strolled the waterfront barefoot, her shoes in hand, laughing softly as the tide lapped at her ankles. She seemed almost free then—not the guarded woman who moved like a ghost among the passengers. Job, standing nearby, realized he was watching more than just a companion on this voyage. He was watching the edge of something he didn't yet understand.

The Roaring Forties

From Ceylon, the *Yeoman* headed south, reaching into the Roaring Forties—those fierce, fast latitudes that circled the bottom of the world. The ship leaned into the wind like a drunk man bracing against a punch. Waves crashed across the bow and froze on the rails. But the speed was glorious. Australia rushed towards them.

Job couldn't shake the weight of McTavish's words. Trouble, the old sailor had warned—and trouble had a name.

Eleanor.

She moved with an air of quiet confidence, her eyes always watching, always measuring. One evening, as Job leaned against the railing, watching the sun bleed into the sea, she appeared beside him.

'You don't trust me, do you?' she asked.

Job turned. 'Should I?'

She smiled, unreadable. 'Trust is a fickle thing on a ship, Mr. Symonds. One moment, you're standing firm. The next, the deck shifts beneath you.'

They spoke of their pasts—Job of Alice, a girl waiting back in Bradwell-on-Sea, and Eleanor of… shadows. Of things left behind, rather than anything she ran toward.

'The sea has a way of changing things, Job Symonds,' she whispered, fingers brushing his arm. 'Best remember that.'

Their encounters grew more frequent, and charged. Eleanor's voice became softer, her words lingered. One night near the hold, as storm winds rose, she stepped close, hand on his chest. 'Not just in the sky,' she said when he spoke of storms.

Job pulled back. 'Goodnight, Eleanor.'

As he walked away, he knew she watched him. Whether with longing or calculation, he couldn't say. The storm—both above and within—was only just beginning.

Secrets in the Hold

As the *Yeoman* crossed into the Indian Ocean, Eleanor's presence grew more purposeful. She lingered near the hatch to the lower decks, whispering to passengers and watching the crew.

One night, Job caught her kneeling by the iron bars of a cell, speaking softly to a convict. 'You shouldn't be here,' she murmured.

'Neither should you,' Job replied. 'Who is he?'

'Someone who doesn't deserve to be in chains.'

'You're planning something. You mean to help him escape.'

'If you tell the captain, he'll hang us both from the yard arm.'

Job wrestled with the weight of it all. The sea's code was clear—but so was the desperation in Eleanor's eyes.

Later that night, Job found her again on deck. Moonlight bathed the sea. 'I know you're plotting something. And I know it involves that man below deck,' he said. 'If you try to free him, you'll doom yourself—and likely half the crew too.'

Eleanor's defiance wavered. 'He doesn't deserve this. I can't just stand by.'

'There's another way,' Job said. 'Work. Stay near the prison. Help him earn a ticket of leave.'

'What's that?'

'An incentive for good behaviour. It lets convicts live and work freely—if they follow the rules and stay in a set place.'

Silence followed, broken only by the creak of the ship.

'You truly believe that's better?'

'I do.'

'Then help me,' she said. 'Not to free him, but to do it right. To find another way.'

And in that moment, a bond was forged—one neither distance nor time would easily sever.

– Landfall

After eighty-four days at sea, land was sighted. The lighthouse on Rottnest Island gave way to Gage Roads off Fremantle where they waited for the pilot to board and take them safely past dangerous reefs and tie up at the long jetty off Fremantle, salt-crusted and weary.

Job stepped off the gangplank with the steady legs of a sailor, but his heart thumped like a drum.

Fifteen thousand miles from the soot and fists of London, he was no longer just a boy from Limehouse. He was a seaman. He was a witness to storms, spices, secrets—and the strange, dangerous tenderness that flickered between himself and Eleanor Briggs.

And ahead, a life in Australia waited.

A land of second chances… or reckoning.

Fremantle

The Long Jetty served Fremantle until 1897 when C.Y. Oconner designed Fremantle harbour and blasted the rock bar at the entrance to allow it to happen.

Shores of Uncertainty

As the *Yeoman* anchored off Fremantle, Job and Eleanor disembarked, eager to explore the burgeoning settlements of Western Australia. The port town of Fremantle buzzed with activity—dockworkers unloaded goods, merchants haggled over prices, and settlers moved with purpose, their eyes set on new beginnings.

Eleanor's gaze swept over the scene, her expression a mix of awe and apprehension. 'It's so different from London,' she murmured.

Job nodded. 'Aye, but there's opportunity here. A chance to start afresh.'

They journeyed inland to Perth, the capital of the Swan River Colony. Established in 1829, Perth had grown steadily, its streets lined with modest buildings and the occasional grand structure, hinting at the prosperity brought by the recent gold rushes.

Their path led them to Mount Eliza, a prominent rise overlooking the city and the winding Swan River. The view from the summit was breathtaking—the expanse of the colony stretched before them, a patchwork of development and untamed wilderness.

Eleanor's eyes glistened as she took in the panorama. 'It's beautiful,' she whispered.

Job glanced at her, a soft smile tugging at his lips. 'It is. A land full of promise.'

Yet, beneath the surface of their exploration, Eleanor grappled with her decision to abandon the perilous plan of freeing William by force. The weight of her choice pressed heavily upon her, and doubt flickered in her eyes.

Sensing her turmoil, Job gently took her hand. 'You're doing the right thing, Eleanor. This path—though longer—is safer for both you and William.'

She turned to him, her resolve wavering. 'But what if it takes years? What if... what if he thinks I've abandoned him?

Job's grip tightened reassuringly. 'He'll understand. And you'll be here, working towards his freedom. Together, we'll find a way.'

Without thinking, Job leaned in, pressing his lips to hers in a tender kiss. For a heartbeat, Eleanor responded, her hand resting on his cheek. Then, reality crashed over them, and she pulled away, eyes wide with confusion.

' I'm sorry,'

Job stammered, stepping back. 'I shouldn't have, your William is in the hold and my Alice is back in England—'

Eleanor shook her head, tears brimming. 'No, it's just... everything is so uncertain. I can't afford to be distracted.'

He nodded, swallowing his own tumultuous feelings. 'Of course. Let's focus on the plan. Albany awaits, and with it, a new beginning.'

They stood side by side atop Mount Eliza, the vast landscape mirroring the uncharted territory of their hearts—beautiful, daunting, and filled with possibilities the bond of friendship building.

Departing Fremantle

The warm air of Fremantle carried the scent of salt and freshly cut timber as Job and Eleanor made their way back to the docks. The time they had spent exploring the town , and journeying inland to Perth had left them both in quiet contemplation. The beauty of the Swan River Colony, the promise of a new world, and the weight of Eleanor's decision had all settled in their minds.

As they walked through the bustling streets, Job stole a glance at Eleanor. She had been distant since their moment atop Mount Eliza, where emotions had overtaken them both. Now, as they neared the waterfront, she let out a deep breath, looking out over the harbor where the *Yeoman* rested in Gage Roads, waiting for the final leg of its journey south.

'You still sure about Albany?' Job asked.

Eleanor nodded slowly. 'Yes. William has a better chance there. It won't be easy, but at least there's hope.'

Job studied her face. The resolve was there, but so was something else—a flicker of doubt, or perhaps the lingering weight of what had passed between them. He wanted to say something, to ease whatever battle she fought inside, but he knew better than to press her now.

As they made their way back towards Fremantle, they passed a gang of convicts working on a dusty road under the watchful eyes of armed guards. Despite their shackles and the heat of the day, the men laughed and joked as they worked, their spirits seemingly undiminished by their circumstances. Eleanor slowed her steps, watching them with a pensive expression.

Job noticed her gaze and nudged her gently. 'See? Life here as a convict isn't all that bad. Hard work, aye, but there's freedom in it. Not every man here is doomed.'

Eleanor said nothing at first, just observing the convicts as they laid stones for the road. Finally, she nodded, though her expression remained clouded. 'I suppose it's not what I imagined.'

As they reached the long jetty where boats ferried supplies and passengers to and from the anchored ships, Eleanor turned to him. 'Job... thank you.'

He gave her a small smile. 'For what'?

She hesitated before answering. 'For talking sense into me. For not letting me make a mistake I couldn't undo.'

Job nodded, but before he could say more, the call came from the jetty: 'Passengers returning to the *Yeoman*, prepare to board!'

They stepped onto the waiting boat, the gentle rock of the waves carrying them back towards the ship. As Fremantle shrank behind them, Eleanor wrapped her arms around herself and exhaled. Job sat beside her, letting the silence between them stretch, knowing that the weight of their decisions would still take time to settle.

As the *Yeoman* prepared to set sail once more, Job cast one last look at the shore. Fremantle had changed something in them both. What lay ahead in Albany would be different, but one thing was certain—their bond, whether they wished for it or not, was now unbreakable.

The Journey to Albany

The *Yeoman* set sail from Fremantle, its bow cutting through the blue waters of the southern coast. The journey to Albany was expected to take around ten days, with the winds favouring them as they moved along the rugged coastline.

With only two convicts left aboard and two guards assigned to them, the atmosphere on deck grew more relaxed. The prisoners, no longer locked below during the day, were allowed time on deck under the watchful but lenient eyes of their overseers who both new of the relationship between William and Eleanor well before now even allowed them the odd hug and kiss. The prisoners were even given tasks—sail repairs, deck scrubbing, and minor maintenance work—to keep them occupied and useful on the voyage.

One afternoon, Job found himself working alongside William Jones

, repairing a damaged yardarm. As they secured the ropes, Job decided to take the opportunity to learn more about the man who had shaped Eleanor's choices.

'You handle tools well,' Job remarked as William expertly tightened a length of cord. 'Must be handy workin' stone and wood.'

William smirked but kept his focus on the task. 'Years of it. I was a stonemason and carpenter back in England. Workin' on a job in London when my luck turned.'

Job adjusted his grip on the spar. 'How'd you find yourself in this predicament'?

William exhaled through his nose, his expression darkening. 'It was a mistake. I'd finished work for the day, packed up my tools, and loaded 'em onto my handcart to take home. Didn't realize I'd left a half-bag of cement on there. The Peelers stopped me, searched my things, and said I was stealin' company property. Before I knew it, I was standin' in court and sentenced to transportation.'

Job frowned. 'All that for half a bag of cement? That doesn't seem right.'

William gave a humourless chuckle. 'Because it aint. Back in the old days, transportation was a way to empty the overcrowded gaols in England. But now? Now the governors in the colonies send the Peelers a list of tradesmen they need, and suddenly, men like me get busted for petty crimes and shipped off to fill the labour shortage.'

Job mulled over William's words. He'd heard tales of unfair sentencing, of men sent across the world for crimes that barely warranted a slap on the wrist. But hearing it firsthand was different.

'That why Eleanor was so desperate to get you out'? Job asked cautiously.

William hesitated, his fingers tightening around the rope. 'Eleanor's got a heart bigger than sense sometimes. She thinks I don't deserve to be here. Maybe she's right, maybe she's wrong. But at least now, she's seeing reason.'

Job nodded. 'She wants to help you earn your freedom the right way. She's fightin' for you, just not in the way she first planned.'

William glanced at Job then, his blue eyes searching. 'And what about you? What's your stake in all this?'

Job hesitated. He could have said it was just about doing the right thing. He could have said it was because he wanted to keep Eleanor from making a mistake. But deep down, he knew it was more than that.

'I just want to see things set right,' Job said simply.

William studied him for a long moment before giving a slow nod. 'Aye. Me too.'

As they finished their work and secured the last of the ropes, Job couldn't help feeling that the days ahead in Albany would bring more than just another port. They would bring choices, challenges, and the shaping of all their futures.

Arrival in Albany

As the *Yeoman* sailed around the heads into Albany, passing the two islands guarding the harbour—Michaelmas and Breaksea—the lighthouse on Breaksea Island stood tall, welcoming them. The water shimmered under the early morning light, revealing the breathtaking sight of Princess Royal Harbour. It was a magnificent natural port, protected and vast, a gateway to what lay ahead for them all.

Eleanor stood at the rail, staring in awe. 'It's beautiful,' she whispered.

Job, standing beside her, nodded. 'Aye. A safe place to land after a long journey. Let's hope it brings safe futures as well.'

As the ship glided towards the docks, the next chapter of their journey—one of labour, hope, and uncertainty—was about to begin.

The passengers and prisoners, along with their guards, disembarked as soon as the *Yeoman* tied up at the dock. The convicts were led off under the supervision of their overseers, though with a far less rigid formality than before. William gave Eleanor a final look before stepping onto the gangplank, disappearing into the growing settlement.

Meanwhile, the crew of the *Yeoman* wasted no time setting to work, unloading goods brought from England—crates of supplies, barrels of provisions, and manufactured goods—before reloading the hold with bales of wool and sacks of wheat bound for the return voyage.

Job knew this was his moment. He had made his decision back in Fremantle, but now came the hard part—telling Captain Mercer that he was leaving the ship.

He found the captain overseeing the reloading process, barking orders to the crew. Job took a steadying breath and approached.

'Captain Mercer, a word, sir?'

Mercer turned, his sharp blue eyes assessing Job. 'Make it quick, Symonds. Plenty of work to do.'

Job squared his shoulders. 'I've decided to stay in Albany, sir. I won't be sailing back with the *Yeoman*.'

The captain's brows lifted, but he didn't look entirely surprised. 'That so? And what's keeping you here, then?'

Job hesitated only a moment before answering. 'Opportunity, sir. A chance at something new.'

Mercer studied him for a long moment, then gave a curt nod. 'Can't say I didn't see it coming. You're a good sailor, Symonds, but you've got more in you than life before the mast. I won't stand in your way.'

Relief washed over Job. 'Thank you, sir.'

Mercer nodded towards the ship. 'You'll be missed aboard. But if you ever find yourself in need of a berth again, I'll see what I can do.'

Job gave the captain a grateful nod before stepping away. As he turned towards the bustling streets of Albany, he felt the weight of his choice settle fully upon him. This was it. A new life awaited him here.

And as he spotted Eleanor in the crowd, watching him with an unreadable expression, he knew that whatever happened next, he wouldn't be facing it alone.

Life begins in the Colony

Exploring Albany

Job and Eleanor stepped into the heart of Albany, eager to explore the opportunities the town had to offer. It was 1887, Albany was a bustling port, strategically positioned as a key coaling station for steam-driven vessels traveling between Britain and Australia. The town's importance had only grown with the signing of a new mail contract that year, ensuring its role in the expanding colonial trade network.

The streets were lined with a mix of stone and timber buildings, housing merchants, ship chandlers, and traders catering to the needs of whalers, settlers, and passing sailors. The scent of the sea mingled with the smoky aroma of coal-burning engines, a reminder of the town's role in fuelling the growing maritime industry.

As they wandered past the market stalls selling fresh produce, salted fish, and leather goods, Eleanor clutched her shawl tightly around her shoulders. The energy of the town was invigorating but also overwhelming. 'I don't know where to start, Job,' she admitted. 'I need work, a place to stay, but everything feels so uncertain.'

Job gave her an encouraging nod. 'We'll figure it out. You're not alone in this.'

They made their way towards the waterfront, where the towering masts of anchored ships swayed gently in the harbor. Dockworkers moved bales of wool and bags of wheat from storage to waiting vessels, preparing cargo for the outbound journeys. The sight of the activity reminded Job of his own position—he had chosen to stay, but now he needed a way to build a life here.

As they passed a group of sailors, Job overheard a conversation that caught his attention.

'Breaksea Lighthouse is short a man,' one of the men was saying. 'Assistant keeper had a nasty fall—won't be back for months. They're looking for a replacement.'

Job stopped in his tracks. A job at a lighthouse—a life by the sea but with steady work—could be exactly what he needed. He turned to Eleanor, excitement flickering in his eyes. 'I think I might have found something.'

Eleanor arched an eyebrow. 'Assistant lighthouse keeper? Sounds lonely.'

Job chuckled. 'Not much different from life aboard ship. And it's honest work. I'll see about it tomorrow.'

Eleanor nodded, a small smile forming. 'That's good, Job. I hope it works out.'

As they continued their exploration, Eleanor also found herself drawn to an opportunity. Near the harbor office a notice board told of a family seeking help for their household—specifically, the Harbour Master's residence, which housed two adults and three children. They needed a maid, someone reliable to assist with domestic duties. Eleanor hesitated at first, but after speaking with the lady of the house, she realized it was a chance to secure a stable position and a roof over her head.

By the time the sun began to set over the harbor, both Job and Eleanor had found potential paths forward. They sat on a wooden bench near the shore, watching the golden light shimmer across the water.

'Strange, isn't it?' Eleanor mused. 'Just days ago, everything felt so uncertain. Now, there's a plan. A way forward.'

Job glanced at her, the wind tousling her hair. 'Aye. A fresh start. Albany might just be the place for it.'

As the last light of day faded into the horizon, they both knew that whatever challenges lay ahead, they had made the right choice in staying.

A Letter to Alice

That night, back in his lodgings, Job sat at a small wooden desk, a single oil lamp casting flickering shadows across the walls. He had always been a man of action rather than words, but tonight, words were all he had. With careful strokes, he dipped the quill into the inkwell and began to write.

Dearest Alice,

I hope this letter finds you well and that you are happy and safe in Bradwell-on-Sea. It has been a long and eventful journey, but I am writing to you now from Albany, Western Australia. I wish you could see this place—it is unlike anything I have ever known. The harbor is magnificent, sheltered by two great islands, and the town itself, though young, is full of promise. Ships from across the world pass through here, and there is a sense that great things are yet to come.

I have found honest work here as an assistant lighthouse keeper on Breaksea Island. The lighthouse stands tall on the rocky cliffs, guiding ships safely into the harbor. It is work that suits me—a place of solitude but also of purpose. Each day brings the sight of the open sea, the sound of the waves crashing against the shore, and the knowledge that I am playing a part in keeping others safe.

Alice, there is something I must say, though I fear my words may not do my heart justice. From the moment I left, not a day has passed that I have not thought of you. The distance between us has only made my feelings clearer. I miss you terribly, and I long for the day when we are no longer apart.

I ask you now, with all the love and sincerity in my heart—will you come to me? Will you join me here in this land of new beginnings, not just as a visitor, but as my wife? I cannot promise riches, nor an easy life, but I can promise you love, devotion, and the chance to build something together.

The sea brought me here, Alice, but it is the thought of you that anchors me. I await your reply with all the hope in my heart.

Yours always,

Job

As he folded the letter and sealed it, Job exhaled, a mixture of nerves and anticipation settling over him. He had not told Alice everything—that in order to rise to full lighthouse keeper, he would need to be married. Nor had he mentioned Eleanor, the woman who had accompanied him on this journey and whose presence had become something of a comfort.

But those were complications for another time. For now, all he could do was send his words across the sea and hope that Alice's heart still belonged to him, as his did to her.

Having carefully folded and sealed the letter, Job knew there was no time to waste. The *Yeoman* was making its final preparations to depart, and if he wanted his letter to reach Alice swiftly, he needed to get it on board.

He hurried through the streets of Albany, his boots kicking up dust as he made his way back to the docks. The ship loomed ahead, its sails partially unfurled, the crew moving efficiently to ready her for the long voyage home. Job climbed aboard and sought out the Chief Officer, who was overseeing the last of the loading.

'Sir,' Job called, slightly out of breath. 'Would you do me a favour? I have a letter—for my Alice. Can you see that it reaches her?'

The officer took the letter and gave Job a knowing smile. 'Aye, Symonds. I'll see it delivered. You take care of yourself out here.'

Job nodded, feeling a mix of relief and longing as he watched the officer tuck the letter safely into his pocket. With a final glance at the *Yeoman*, his last connection to England, he turned and stepped back onto the dock, watching as the ship began to ease away from the shore.

His letter was now on its way, carrying with it the weight of his heart and the hope of a future he could only dream of.

The tavern was quieter than usual that evening, the soft murmur of conversation wrapping itself around the low-beamed ceiling like an old, familiar shawl. A fire smouldered in the hearth, and the scent of bread fresh from the oven mingled with the sharper tang of spilled ale and sea salt from the wharf outside.

Job sat at a corner table, a simple meal laid out before him—stew thick with barley and root vegetables, a crusty loaf, and a mug of dark beer. Eleanor slipped into the seat opposite with a small smile, brushing a strand of hair from her brow. No need for pleasantries; between them, words often took second place to the easy understanding that had long grown between their hearts.

For a moment, Job simply studied her, committing the sight of her to memory. In another life, perhaps—but not in this one. Their bond was something different, something no proposal or promise could replace.

'I sent it,' Job said at last, breaking the bread in two and offering her a piece.

Eleanor's eyes softened. She did not need to ask what 'it' was. She already knew.. She always knew the workings of Job's heart better than most.

'To Alice,' she said, her voice steady but warm.

He nodded, feeling the weight of it settle a little lighter now that it was spoken aloud. 'Aye. She'll have it in a few months—or near enough.'

They ate in companionable silence for a few minutes, the fire crackling low beside them. Then Eleanor leaned back in her chair, regarding him with a look that was part mischief, part affection.

'Well, it's about time,' she teased gently. 'You've been carrying her in your pocket long enough.'

Job chuckled, a low, rough sound that made a few nearby heads turn before returning to their own business. 'I reckon I have at that.'

A brief shadow crossed Eleanor's face—gone so quickly Job might have missed it, if he hadn't known her so well. But she only reached for her mug and raised it slightly in salute.

'To bold hearts and long voyages,' she said.

Job lifted his own in return. 'And to the friends who see us on our way.'

Their mugs clinked together softly.

Outside, the evening mist rolled in from the harbour, wrapping the town in a damp hush. Inside, for one quiet, perfect moment, two old souls sat together—no promises, no regrets. Only the quiet acknowledgment of all they had been to each other, and all they would remain, even as the next chapter of Job's life beckoned from across the water at Breaksea Island.

He would leave soon. But for now, there was bread to break, a fire to share, and the company of someone who, in her own steadfast way, had always been family.

Journey to Breaksea Island

The following morning, Job stood at the docks just as the first light of dawn crept over the horizon. The supply boat to Breaksea Island was preparing to depart, its deck loaded with barrels, crates, and sacks of provisions—monthly supplies for the lighthouse keeper and his wife.

At precisely 7 a.m., the boat pushed off, heading into the open waters of King George Sound. The twelve-mile journey to Breaksea Island was a steady one, passing through the sheltered waters of Princess Royal Harbour before entering the more exposed stretches of sea beyond. The water was calm that morning, a blessing Job was grateful for as he stood near the bow, inhaling the salt air.

As the island loomed ahead, Job caught sight of the Breaksea Lighthouse perched high above the rocky cliffs. Access to the island was no simple feat—once the boat reached the first landing, Job had to climb a rope ladder to the lower platform before being hoisted up in a bosun's chair, a process that was also used for lifting supplies.

As he finally stepped onto the solid wooden jetty, he was met by the lighthouse keeper and his wife. The keeper, a weathered man with sharp eyes and a stiff demeanour, eyed Job with mild scepticism.

'Symonds, is it?' the keeper said gruffly. 'You've no experience keeping a light, do you?'

'No, sir,' Job admitted, straightening his shoulders. 'But I'm willing to learn.'

The keeper let out a huff, arms crossed. 'We'll see about that. It's not a sailor's job—this is work that never stops. Light needs trimming, glass needs cleaning, and you'll be keeping records every day. You up for it?'

Job nodded without hesitation. 'Aye, sir. I wouldn't be here if I wasn't.'

The keeper studied him a moment longer before giving a short nod. 'Good. We'll start with unloading these supplies. Then you'll see what you've got yourself into.'

As Job set to work, hauling provisions up from the landing with the islands donkey, he felt the full weight of the new life ahead of him. It would be hard, unforgiving work, but it was honest. And for the first time in a long while, he felt as though he was truly building something for himself.

The boat slipped away, its oars flashing once, twice, then vanishing into the mist that clung to Breaksea like an old, tattered shawl. Job stood on the rocky ledge above the landing, his kit bag slung over one shoulder, a bundle of oilskins under the other, and watched until the faint sound of rowlocks faded into silence.

The island breathed around him — a low, salt-wet sigh of wind through the hardy shrubs, the endless crash of waves against the granite spine of the land. It was a lonely sound, but not unfriendly. A hard place, perhaps, but a fair one, if a man was willing to meet it halfway.

The head keeper, old McGuire, waited a few paces up the path. 'No dawdlin', lad. Time and tide won't wait for your dreams.'
His voice was rough but not unkind. Like the island, Job thought — harsh on the outside, maybe, but holding something steady and good underneath.

He followed McGuire up the track to the lighthouse, its bright white tower standing sentinel against the grey sky. There, Job's real work would begin.

The days found their rhythm quickly.

Up before dawn to check the lamp and the weather; days spent mending the stonework, polishing brass, keeping the mighty lens spotless. Every week, a logbook to complete, tides to chart, machinery to oil, rope and timber to mend. Supplies came once a month — assuming the weather didn't keep the boat at bay — and always there was the light to tend, the endless, patient light.

There was company of a sort: McGuire, grumbling into his pipe; young Dawson, who said little but played a fine fiddle when he thought no one was listening; and Simmons, a broad-shouldered fellow from Albany who always had a joke ready, though most were poor enough to make a cat laugh.

But the island itself was the truest companion. It spoke in the crash of surf and the shriek of gulls, the hiss of the wind around the lantern room, the creak of timbers settling in the damp.
And in the quiet, Job's thoughts turned again and again to Alice.

At night, after the lamp was trimmed and checked, Job often found himself sitting on the low wall outside the keeper's cottage, staring out over the dark water. McGuire would join him, pipe smoke curling into the damp air.

'Thinkin' of yer girl again?' McGuire asked one evening, his voice soft for once.

Job gave a small shrug. 'Aye. Wonderin' if she'll come.'

McGuire sucked on his pipe, considering. 'Women've got more pluck than we give 'em credit for, lad. If she's half the measure you say, she'll find her way.'

Job smiled into the dark. 'She's better than I deserve.'

McGuire chuckled dryly. 'Ain't we all, boy. Ain't we all.'

The months dragged on.

Spring bled into summer, fierce and dry. Summer moved into autumn, wet and chill. Winter returned with storms that shook the stones of the lighthouse and sent spray flying higher than the lantern windows. Still no word.

Between duties, conversation drifted over many things.

One evening, as the wind rattled the shutters, McGuire tapped the newspaper he'd saved from the last supply run.

'Big trouble up north. Broome took a right hammerin'.'
He handed the scrap to Job, who scanned the bold type: *Cyclone lashes Broome — many feared dead.*

'Lost half the pearling fleet, they reckon,' McGuire said grimly. 'Poor devils never stood a chance. Seas rose twenty foot, tore whole houses apart.'

Job shook his head. 'So much taken by the sea... without warnin'.'

McGuire knocked out his pipe. 'Warnin's for them that listen. Trouble is, most men think they've got more time than they do.'

They sat in silence a while, the words heavy between them.

At Christmas, the keepers shared a rough meal of salt beef and tinned fruit, passing around a dented flask of whiskey under the moan of the winter wind. Job managed a smile, but later, sitting alone on the rocky point, he let the sadness wash over him.

Had she forgotten him? Had the silence been her answer?

There were nights he lay awake, listening to the wind clawing at the shutters, and wondered if he was a fool.

Perhaps the old sea-dogs were right — the sea took as much as it gave.

Later in the new year, when summer crept back and the air grew heavy with the scent of salt and wildflowers, McGuire brought another scrap of news.

'Talk down at Albany is about a new Constitution,' he said, spitting into the grass. 'Want to tie the colonies together — one nation, they're sayin'.'

Job leaned against the wall, arms folded. 'One nation, eh? Might be we'd stand stronger against the rest o' the world.'

McGuire gave a snort. 'Might be we'll just argue louder, with more fools round the table. Still,' he added, 'Better to be brothers than strangers.'

Job thought about it long after McGuire had gone back inside.
Maybe the world was changing faster than he'd thought — ships bigger, ports busier, new countries rising where old ones faded.

And somewhere in that wide, restless world, Alice was reading his words, deciding her course.

Then, one brittle morning late in August, with the wind still carrying a breath of winter, the supply boat came.

Job stood by the jetty, oilskins flapping, helping haul the barrels of oil and sacks of flour ashore. He wasn't expecting anything. Hope had grown thin over the long months, worn almost to transparency.

Then Simmons came striding up, a grin splitting his weathered face.

'Got somethin' fer ye, Symonds,' he said, waving a crumpled, salt-streaked envelope.

Job took it with hands that trembled, hardly daring to believe.

The handwriting was unmistakable. Neat, careful, full of the grace he remembered — and his name written as though she had spoken it softly when the ink was still wet.

He climbed away from the bustle of the landing, up to the high rocks overlooking the southern ocean. There, he sat with the letter resting in his palm like a living thing.

The seal cracked. The paper unfolded.

And the words — her words — tumbled out, warming him better than any hearth fire.

She had received his letter. She had thought long and hard. She missed him — terribly, achingly. And if he would have her, if he was still sure, then she would come to him.
She would come to Australia.

My Dearest Job,

Oh, what joy it was to receive your letter! I read it over and over again, scarcely believing the words before me. My heart has longed for you more than I can say, and to know that you have made a home in this distant land, fills me with both pride and sorrow. Pride, because you are building a future with such determination, and sorrow, because I have missed you so dearly.

Your proposal has taken my breath away, and I can say nothing but yes, a thousand times yes! I would be honoured to be your wife, Job. To stand beside you and build a life together in this strange and wonderful new land. I am overjoyed by the thought of it and humbled by your love.

Yet, I must confess that I do not know when I can join you. Passage to Australia is not an easy thing for a woman alone, and while I have inquired about ships bound for Albany, I have not yet secured a berth. But rest assured, my love, I will come to you as soon as I can. I will not let time nor distance stand in the way of what we both desire.

As I write this, I think of Bradwell-on-Sea and all the places that once felt like home. And yet, none of them truly are anymore, not without you. I have waited long enough for happiness, and at twenty-eight, some call me an old maid, but I care not for their words. My future lies with you, and I will not waver.

Please write to me as soon as you receive this, and tell me all that you can—of your work, your days, of Albany and its people. And of course, tell me once more that you love me, for I never tire of hearing it.

Job read the letter three times before leaning back in his chair, his heart swelling. She was coming to him—perhaps not today, perhaps not next month, but she would come. And that was enough.

He stepped outside, inhaling the salt air, looking across the endless stretch of ocean. Somewhere beyond the horizon, Alice was waiting for her moment to set sail.

And when she did, he would be ready for her.

Job bowed his head against the rising wind, the letter cradled to his chest, his shoulders shaking not with the cold but with a fierce, quiet joy.

The island could keep its storms and its silence.
The sea could take what it liked.

But for now, against all odds, the wind was at his back — and somewhere out there, across the vastness of the world Alice was coming.

The next morning, as Job was hauling a crate of kerosene up to the lantern room, McGuire found him.

The old man leaned against the stone wall, watching with that shrewd, weather-beaten gaze of his. He said nothing at first, just struck a match and lit his pipe, letting the smoke drift between them.

Finally, he grunted.
'Saw ye up on the rocks yesterday. Looked like a man who just found gold where he thought there was nothin' but stones.'

Job wiped his hands on his trousers, trying to hide the foolish grin that kept tugging at his mouth. 'Aye,' he said, voice thick. 'She's comin'. Alice... she's comin' to Australia.'

McGuire nodded slowly, as if he had expected no less.

He puffed on his pipe, then tapped the bowl out against his boot.
'Well, lad,' he said, his voice gentler than Job had ever heard it, 'when she gets here, you hang onto her.'

He jabbed a thick finger towards Job's chest, the gesture rough but strangely tender. 'Hang onto her with both hands. Don't let the sea, nor work, nor foolish pride get between you. Life's got a thousand ways to pull folks apart if you let it.'

Job swallowed hard, the salt air stinging his eyes more than usual. 'I will,' he said. 'I swear it.'

McGuire grunted approval — but his brow furrowed slightly, and he leaned in, lowering his voice.
'And listen sharp, lad. If ye mean to wed her out here — on Breaksea — you'll need more than just good intentions.'

Job blinked, caught off guard.

'You'll have to write to the Governor for special permission,' McGuire said, thumbing tobacco into his pipe again.
'They don't take kindly to lighthouses bein' turned into wedding chapels without say-so.'

He struck a match and continued, the flame lighting the deep lines of his face.

'And you'll need a minister — and a boat — and a proper oarsman to fetch her out. Weather's fickle 'round here. Best not leave it to the last minute.'

Job felt the weight of it settle on him — the realisation that loving her wasn't enough; he had to prepare, had to fight for the life he wanted.

'I'll see to it,' he said firmly.

McGuire gave a nod, approving.
'Good. Plan it proper, Symonds. A man's only as good as the promises he keeps.'

Then he straightened, slapped Job once on the shoulder — hard enough to stagger him — and turned away, his oilskins flapping in the wind.

As he climbed the narrow track back to the tower, Job stood alone for a moment longer, the crate forgotten at his feet, feeling the weight of the old man's words settle into him — solid, steady, like the stones of the lighthouse itself.

The light above him turned in its endless, tireless circle, casting its beam far across the restless sea.

A signal.
A promise.
A home worth fighting for.

Securing Her Passage

For Alice Cook of Maldon, Essex, securing a berth to Australia was no easy feat. Many ships made the long voyage, but few had room for an unattached woman traveling alone. Though she inquired at the docks in London, passage proved expensive, and captains were hesitant to take on single women without family or patronage.

Months passed, and though her determination never wavered, frustration grew. Then, by chance, an opportunity arose.

A prominent Irish engineer, C.Y. O'Connor, had been appointed as Western Australia's Engineer-in-Chief. He was gathering his family and household for the voyage to Perth, where he would take up his new position.

He had been working in New Zealand and was home on a break when he received an offer from Premier John Forrest to take charge of all Rail, Harbours, Water supplies ,everything, it was a fantastic opportunity full of challenge on which O'Conner thrived as long as he was in control he could move mountains and he accepted the offer immediately.

They required a governess for their children—someone of good standing, educated, and capable of managing lessons and discipline during the long journey.

Through a friend of a friend, Alice heard of the opportunity and wasted no time in applying. She presented herself to O'Connor's wife, a woman of sharp wit and keen judgment. Alice spoke of her education, her experience, and her ability to manage young children. But most importantly, she spoke of her desire to travel to Albany.

Mrs. O'Connor studied her for a long moment before nodding. 'You are well-spoken and seem capable enough. The voyage will be long and sometimes difficult. You must be prepared for that.'

Alice nodded firmly. 'I am prepared for whatever is necessary, ma'am.'

That was enough. Within days, she found herself aboard a well-fitted steamer, her passage secured as part of the O'Connor household.

Alice boarded the *RMS Oroya* with a mixture of terror and resolve. She was not a seasoned traveller. Her only sea journey thus far had been trips with Dad to London in the Thames Barge and the ferry to France, once, with an aunt who disapproved of everything.

But this was different. She had letters from Job—tender, teasing, full of promise. She had the blessing of a cousin, a half-smile from her mother, and a trunk full of proper clothing for a new life. She was going to Australia. Not to escape, but to follow her heart.

Her relationship with the O'Connor family had settled into a polite, if slightly tense rhythm. Mrs. O'Connor was measured and efficient, and the children well-behaved enough under Alice's care. But it was Mr. O'Connor—Charles—who occasionally made her wince. Brilliant though he clearly was, his temperament could swing like a compass in a storm. At the slightest delay or inconvenience, his voice would rise, sharp and clipped, with a brooding energy that made Alice stiffen. There was no cruelty in him, but something tightly wound, like a machine under pressure. Alice found herself treading carefully, mindful not to provoke one of his outbursts. He meant well, she was sure—

but he was a man driven by the weight of great expectations, and sometimes, it showed more than he knew.

There were moments, late at night when the children had gone quiet and the lamps flickered low, that Alice glimpsed something deeper in Mr O'Conner. He would stand alone at the rail, staring out at the endless water, his fingers twitching at his cuffs, as if wrestling with invisible calculations or burdens too vast to voice. Once, she overheard him muttering about delays and pressures from 'those in Perth'—his tone dark, his posture tight. Alice, watching quietly from the shadows, though if fate struck him in just the right place, he might shatter.

The ship was a steam-assisted liner, tall and confident, and it followed the same route as Job's had done only a few years before—through the Mediterranean, and then into the marvel of the modern world: the Suez Canal.

Port Said was a wonder. Alice stayed mostly aboard, but she watched from the rail as the ship passed Arab dhows and French gunboats, saw children run barefoot along the water's edge, and gasped when the domes of mosques gleamed in the setting sun. The transition from the calm Mediterranean to the sweltering Suez was a trial, but she managed it with decorum.

Aden, by contrast, shocked her. It was dusty, hot, and utterly foreign. She was offered incense and ivory combs by traders who spoke five languages and smiled without meaning it. She refused them all, clinging to her parasol as if it might anchor her to England.

But in Colombo, her spirit lifted. She adored the colour, the birdsong, the distant chime of temple bells. A Ceylonese woman with bright bangles gifted her a small garland of frangipani as she returned to the ship. It withered by morning, but Alice kept it anyway, pressed between the pages of *Persuasion*.

The final leg of the journey was brutal. The Roaring Forties lived up to their name— roaring with wind and slicing cold. The *RMS Oroya* leaned deep into the swell, racing eastward across the Southern Ocean. On one frightful night, a great wave broke over the decks, and Alice, clutching her prayer book, whispered Job's name into the dark.

But finally—Fremantle, and then Albany.

It looked rough and new—little more than a dusty settlement with stout men and fewer women. But the moment she stepped onto the dock, every fear melted.

She was finally on her way to Job.

She was home.

By now, Job was a seasoned veteran of lighthouse keeping. His dedication had not gone unnoticed, and with his impending marriage, he was granted larger quarters on Breaksea Island. With only weeks to prepare, he set about making their new home comfortable for Alice's arrival.

Knowing that he would need skilled hands to help him ready the cottage, Job sent word to the Harbourmaster requesting the assistance of a carpenter. When the work crew arrived, Job stepped outside to greet them—and stopped in his tracks.

Standing among the men, tool bag slung over his shoulder, was none other than William, the convict partner of Eleanor.

For a moment, neither man spoke. Then, William smirked. 'Didn't expect to see me again, did you?'

Job crossed his arms. 'Not particularly. Last I saw you, you were off to serve your sentence.'

William wiped the sweat from his brow. 'Aye, that I was. But good behaviour and a skill in demand get you far in this colony. They've put me to work on government projects. Seems a man who knows his way around timber and stone is worth keeping busy.'

As they walked towards the cottage, William added, 'I've been given a special commission—stone masonry work on the new town hall. It's the most important work I've done yet. The officials tell me that if I do a fine job, I'll be granted my ticket of leave. That means I'll be free to work for myself, start my own business… and finally marry Eleanor.'

Job listened, a small smile playing at his lips. 'That's good news, William. Sounds like you've got your own fresh start ahead.'

William nodded. 'Aye. There are conditions, of course. I'll have to present myself at the police station regularly, attend church on Sundays, and I can't leave the area without permission. But it's freedom, of a kind. And it means Eleanor and I can marry and build a life here.'

Job clapped him on the shoulder. 'Then let's get to work. Alice will be here soon, and this place needs to be ready.'

As they set to work, the past seemed to fade away, replaced by the task at hand. Job had spent years imagining this day—preparing a home for Alice, building a life in a land he had once known nothing about. And now, as the walls of his future came together under William's skilled hands, the reality of it all began to sink in.

Alice was coming. And this time, he was truly ready for her , He had spent all his spare time building a bonfire on the seaward side of the island, collecting anything flammable he could to welcome her. He had received the special approval from Governor Sir Frederick Broome to marry Alice on the Island , the minister, the boat and the oarsman had been organised, and Job boasted to William of his organisational prowess.

Job stood on the rocky ledge above the landing, arms folded, boots tapping an impatient rhythm against the stone. The lightkeeper's tower loomed behind him, the sea stretched restless and wide before him — but all Job could see in his mind's eye was the little boat that would soon be rowing towards them, carrying Alice.

He straightened his jacket for the third time that hour, checking the knots on the small flag he'd hoisted — white cloth with a blue stripe, the signal to guide them in.

Behind him, a familiar voice drawled,

'Well, well, look at *Captain Important* over here.'

Job turned to see William grinning broadly, hands shoved deep in his pockets, an eyebrow cocked.

'Heard ye pulled every string from here to Perth,' William went on, smirking. 'Permission from the Governor, a preacher roped in from town, a boat chartered like you're some grand toff expectin' a royal parade.'

Job flushed a little, but tried to keep his dignity. 'Had to be done proper.'

'Aye, *proper*,' William teased, stepping closer and giving Job a light thump on the arm. 'Remind me to bow and doff me cap when she steps ashore, yer lordship.'

Job gave a low chuckle, shaking his head.

William softened then, his grin turning genuine.

'Truth is, Job, I reckon Alice is a lucky woman. Not every man'd move heaven and earth just to make sure the weddin' went right.'

He clapped Job on the shoulder, firm and warm.

'Now just don't go cockin' it all up by blubberin' like a big soft fool when you see her, eh?'

Job laughed — a rich, relieved sound that whipped away across the salty air.

'No promises,' he said.

They stood together a moment longer, two rough men facing the vastness of the sea, hearts steady, a little battered, but filled with hope.

And out beyond the breakers, somewhere, a small boat was already making its way towards them.

Alice's Arrival

Alice adjusted the brim of her feathered hat, the faded plumage fluttering as the breeze swept in off the harbour. It wasn't exactly a wedding hat—certainly not the kind she'd imagined wearing—but it was all she had, and she wore it with quiet determination.

The wooden planks of Albany's harbour creaked underfoot as she stepped towards the dinghy bobbing at the pier. A weathered oarsman, his face carved by sun and salt, steadied the vessel with one hand and tipped his cap with the other.

'Ready for the crossing, miss'?

Alice nodded, her gloved fingers bunching the hem of her simple grey silk dress. 'As ready as I'll ever be.'

Beside her, the Wesleyan minister offered his arm, his expression gentle as he helped her into the unsteady boat. Alice accepted with a soft smile, lowering herself onto the narrow bench as the oarsman shoved off from the wharf with a practiced grunt. The skiff rocked as they drifted into the channel, the town of Albany shrinking slowly behind them.

The salt air filled Alice's lungs, crisp and bracing. Her gaze swept across King George Sound, the open stretch of water that lay between her and Breaksea Island—her new home.

She reached instinctively to the hidden sachet tucked safely within her bodice, feeling the crinkle of paper and the delicate remains of the wild rose Job had given her years before, back in their English village. The petals were brittle now, almost dust, but she clung to them as if they were gold.

It had been three long years since Job had boarded a ship to Australia, chasing the promise of a better life. Three years of silence, aching questions, and her father's increasingly desperate attempts to marry her off.

'You're not getting any younger, Alice,' he'd grumbled more than once. 'That blacksmith down the lane is still interested.'

She had shuddered at the thought. 'He's twice my age and smells like soot!'

Her father had only shaken his head. 'You're twenty-five. You're lucky to have any offers.'

But fate had intervened with one handwritten letter that changed everything. Job's voice had leapt off the page—full of stories about wide skies, wild weather, and a solitary island where the sea crashed against black rocks and the stars felt close enough to touch. He'd written of his longing, his hope, and, most of all, his love.

He had asked her to come.

Now, here she was, crossing the vast harbour towards a rocky speck in the sea.

'How far is it to the island?' she asked the oarsman as the waves slapped against the sides of the skiff.

'Twelve miles, give or take. The weather's on our side today. Shouldn't be more than four or so hours'

Alice looked ahead, trying to make out the shape of Breaksea Island. In the distance, a sea eagle spiralled overhead. She thought of the bonfire Job had lit two days before, when her ship from England passed the island. She hadn't seen him clearly from the deck, but the blaze had been unmistakable—huge and bright, built with love and back-breaking labour. It had lit a fire in her heart, too, one that had carried her through these final days of uncertainty.

The little boat pitched slightly as they passed the craggy shore of Point King Lighthouse.
Children clambered up the rocks, waving their hats and kerchiefs, their shouts of encouragement whipped away by the brisk sea breeze.
One woman cupped her hands around her mouth and hollered, 'You're nearly there!' — her voice carrying strong and clear across the water.

Another woman, apron fluttering in the wind, held up a small posy of wildflowers as if to offer Alice a welcome from the shore.
From the cliff path above, a ripple of applause broke out — scattered, spontaneous, but full of warmth — as mothers and daughters, aunties and grandmothers watched the tiny boat press bravely onward.

They knew.
All of Albany seemed to know by now — of the young woman from England who had crossed the world for love, and the lighthouse man who waited for her out on Breaksea.

Their story had become *everyone's story* — a rare bright thread woven through the hard, weathered fabric of their little town.

And as the dinghy pulled steadily towards the open stretch beyond the headland, the women and children at Point King watched with shining eyes, some whispering prayers, others smiling through sudden, unexpected tears.

Alice caught the sounds and sights through the salt spray, blinking against the brightness.
The children's laughter, the women's cheers, the distant flutter of handkerchiefs — all of it blurred together in her mind, filling her chest with a strange, aching joy.
Every pull of the oars, every slap of the sea against the hull, brought her closer to him — to the man who had waited, and hoped, and built a place for her on that lonely, shining rock ahead.

From his lookout atop the rocky bluff, Job caught the first glimpse of the dinghy as it rounded the headland — a tiny black speck bobbing against the endless shimmer of the sea.

His heart leapt so hard he had to grip the rail to steady himself.
That was her.
That was Alice.

He shaded his eyes with one hand, leaning forwards as though he could pull the little boat closer by will alone.
Every stroke of the oars brought it nearer, the small hull dipping and rising against the restless chop of the bay.

A fresh gust of wind kicked up a scatter of whitecaps, and Job's gut twisted.
Was she getting soaked out there?
The salt spray would ruin her dress — and she'd spent good money on it, no doubt, wanting to look her best.
Worse — what if the swell turned rougher halfway across the open water?
He knew that feeling — the sudden lurch, the sour turn in the stomach — and the thought of Alice, pale and miserable in the bottom of the dinghy, made him pace three steps forwards and back, muttering under his breath.

'Come on, lad, easy strokes now,' he urged aloud, though they were still too far to hear him.

He caught himself laughing softly — a short, breathless sound.
In all the years he'd worked the tides, tended the lamp and battled storms, he'd never felt so utterly, hopelessly helpless as he did now, watching the woman he loved inch towards him across a sea he could not tame.

And yet, she was coming.
She was coming.

Alice clung to the sides of the skiff as another wave splashed over the bow, blotting the hem of her silk dress. She laughed in spite of herself.

The oarsman tightened his grip on the worn handles as the little dinghy began to lift and lurch against the rougher chop beyond the point.
He cast a quick glance at the young woman seated amidships — pale, clutching her skirts against the spray — and muttered under his breath, not unkindly,
'Brave lass... not many'd fancy this stretch in a Sunday dress.'

He set his shoulders to the oars, muscles straining steady against the swell.
There was no turning back now.
One way or another, they were bound for Breaksea.

'Well, that's the first part of me soaked,' she said, gripping her hat.

The minister chuckled. 'Never mind the gown, Miss Alice. You're nearly a married woman, and you're braver than most I know.'

It wasn't long before the outline of a cottage around the lighthouse appeared—whitewashed walls nestled high on the island, with a string of bunting snapping in the breeze. Alice stared. Could that be their cottage? Job had promised a home, but the sight of it made it real.

As the skiff pulled into a calm cove on the lee side of the island, the oarsman pointed towards a rope ladder hanging down from the landing high above the water.

'Climb that, and there's a chair rigged to haul you up the last stretch to the jetty,' he said. 'Bit of a rugged welcome, but that's island life.'

Alice steadied her nerves and her skirts, glancing up the cliff. Her heart thudded.

Then she heard him.

'ALICE!'

There, waving with both arms and grinning like a schoolboy, stood Job.

His face was leaner now, his skin tanned and weathered, but that grin—that grin was still hers.

She climbed with shaking limbs, and when Job finally reached down and took her hands, the world fell away.

He pulled her into his arms on the creaking wooden jetty, breathless and damp from sea spray. Gulls screeched above them, the wind whipped around their ears, but all she heard was the rush of his voice.

'Welcome home, love.'

And for the first time in a long while, Alice truly believed she was.
But then her eyes followed the zigzagging path up the steep hill and beyond, across the ridges to where the lighthouse stood sentinel against the sky.

'Job,' she said, shading her eyes against the sun, 'how far is it?'

''Bout a mile,' he replied with a grin.

'Blimey,' Alice muttered, adjusting her skirts, 'I didn't expect such a difficult climb.'

'You'll be all right, love,' Job said, offering his hand with a reassuring smile. 'And the donkey will carry your valise.'

Alice gave a weary laugh, grateful for Job's steadying presence — and for the sure-footed little beast waiting patiently by the track.

Job and Alice in Australia

A Wedding on the Edge of the World

They set off slowly, making their way up the narrow, winding path. The steep zigzag climb tested them all, each step a careful negotiation between loose stones and the pull of the sea wind. At the top, the trail flattened along a rocky ridge, leading them onward towards the lighthouse, where the keeper and his wife stood waiting, small figures against the vastness of sky and ocean.

Alice stood beside Job, her damp grey silk dress clinging to her from the sea spray of the journey across. The wind whistled around them, tugging at veils and hair, while the crashing waves below the jetty served as the only accompaniment to the solemn voice of the Wesleyan minister.

Alice couldn't help finding it strange — almost comical, in its way — that he began with the formal words, 'Dearly beloved, we are gathered here today…'

when their entire congregation consisted only of the lighthouse keeper, his wife, the oarsman who had rowed her ashore, and of course, themselves.

Her mind flickered, unbidden, to the last church service she had attended — a grand affair in London, where nearly a thousand souls had packed the pews, their voices rising like a mighty chorus beneath the vaulted stone ceiling. How different it was here, standing on a remote island with only the endless sky and roaring sea as witnesses to this new beginning.

.

Still, the weight of the moment was not lost on her. Job's weatherworn face held the same steady determination she had loved for years, and as she took his hands, she knew that her life had forever changed. When the vows were spoken and the minister finally declared them husband and wife, Job leaned in and kissed her—gently at first, then with a growing urgency that made her blush in the presence of their small audience.

The minister and oarsman walked back down the path and left in the dingy, the lighthouse keeper went back to work.

Job and Alice walked together up towards the lighthouse cottage, Job eager to show her the place that was now her home. He led her across the rocky island, pointing out the burrows of the mutton birds. 'These,' he explained, along with rabbits 'will be part of our diet. Their eggs are rich, and when the birds are plump, they make a fine meal.'

Alice wrinkled her nose at the thought but said nothing. Then, he gestured to the patches of rough green plants growing in a sheltered corner near the cottage. 'Stinging nettles,' he said. 'Once our vegetables from Albany start to wilt and rot, we use these as greens. If you know how to prepare them, they make a decent meal.'

Alice recoiled instinctively, staring at the weeds with dismay. 'Surely you jest, Job?'

He chuckled. 'No jesting, love. The supply boat only comes once a month. We eat what we have, we catch some fish but often its mutton bird stew or eggs or rabbits we trap. We do have a goat to milk. That will be your task lass; Ill teach you how.

She swallowed hard, realising for the first time just how different life here would be. But she had not come all this way to complain. If this was to be her home, she would learn its ways. 'Then you'll have to teach me how to make something decent from all of this.'

'That's my Alice,' Job said, beaming at her.

That evening, Alice did her best with their first dinner together as husband and wife. With a bit of salted meat from the stores and some root vegetables still fresh enough to eat, she managed to cook something hearty. She wasn't ready to add mutton bird or nettles to the mix just yet, but she knew the time would come.

After the meal, Job reached for her hand and led her nervously to the small bedroom in the cottage. The wind still howled outside, but inside, the air was warm with the heat of the lamp. They had lain together before, always holding back, fearful of an untimely pregnancy before marriage. But now, there was no hesitation in Alice. As Job pulled her into his arms, she welcomed his touch, her body pressed against his, their long years of waiting finally behind them.

Tonight, their life together truly began.

As the days passed, Alice slowly adapted to life on Breaksea Island. The isolation was daunting, but Job ensured she had plenty to occupy her mind. One of the first things he taught her was how to use semaphore flags.

'Ships pass by more often than you'd think,' Job explained, standing beside her on the rocky outcrop where messages were usually sent. 'If we need to communicate with them, semaphore is the fastest way.'

Alice grasped the small wooden-handled flags, mirroring Job's movements as he demonstrated. It was challenging at first, but with time, she found it almost enjoyable, the rhythm of the signals giving her a strange sense of control over the vast sea around them.

Job, too, had his own studies to tend to. He was determined to earn his Harbour Pilot's ticket, which required more learning than he had ever done in his life. Alice, ever the diligent student, helped him prepare by quizzing him on charts, navigational rules, and weather patterns.

'We'll make a system of it,' she proposed one day, smiling. 'I'll ask you questions in semaphore while you're in the lighthouse, and you can answer in Morse code. That way, even while working, you're studying, and it will help me perfect my semaphore.'

Job laughed but agreed—it was a fine plan, and soon their exchanges across the island became routine. Alice would stand outside, signalling her questions, and Job, high up in the lantern room, would tap out his replies in Morse with the clank of his tools.

Four months into their marriage, Alice began to feel different—more tired than usual, with an odd sense of queasiness in the mornings. The realization struck her suddenly, and when she finally told Job, his face lit up with pure joy.

'A child!' he exclaimed, pulling her close. 'Alice, we're going to have a child!'

At thirty she had quietly feared that the chance of motherhood had passed her by. But now, she knew that their little family was growing. Due in mid-1890, they speculated about whether it would be a boy or a girl. 'Well, I suppose we'll just have to wait until the little one arrives to find out,' Job said with a grin.

Together, they discussed names. If it was a boy, they would name him Henry Homer, after Job's father. If a girl, she would be called Ella Bessie a name Alice had always loved.

As the months stretched on, Alice continued to learn the ways of the island, and Job worked harder than ever to provide for his growing family. The lighthouse stood as a silent guardian over them, and as the waves crashed against the shore, the two of them prepared for the next great adventure—parenthood.

Life on Breaksea Island

Life on Breaksea Island settled into a rhythm, one dictated by the tides, the weather, and the ever-present needs of the lighthouse. The passing of ships became an event that broke up the isolation, and Alice grew used to standing with Job as he signalled messages to passing vessels. She learned to recognize the different flags of merchant ships, whalers, and naval steamers. Some captains, recognizing the lighthouse keepers' reliance on outside supplies, occasionally sent parcels of fresh fruit or a newspaper down with their skiffs, small tokens that reminded Job and Alice they were not entirely alone in the world.

Birds were everywhere—mutton birds, gulls, and even albatross, their wings spanning wider than Alice's outstretched arms. Their cries filled the air, sometimes deafening, sometimes comforting. The mutton birds, with their burrows tucked into the island's grassy slopes, became a valuable food source, though Alice still struggled with the idea of eating them. Job, accustomed to the harsh necessities of island life, assured her they were nourishing, and after enough hunger, she relented, learning how to prepare them in a way that made them more palatable.

Their diet, while limited, was manageable. Salted meat and hardtack formed the backbone of their pantry, supplemented by whatever they could gather or receive from the supply boat. Job had managed to cultivate a small garden of hardy vegetables— onions, carrots, and even a few struggling potatoes. Alice, determined to make the best of it, experimented in the kitchen, trying different ways to prepare their meagre rations into something resembling comfort food. She became an expert at catching Rabbit or Mutton birds to supplement their diet.

Life as a married couple had its own ebb and flow. Some days were blissful—Job would take Alice by the hand and lead her along the rocky coastline, pointing out the shifting sandbars and the hidden currents that only a keen sailor's eye could detect. Other days, frustrations arose. The isolation, the monotony of chores, and the ever-present wind wore on Alice's nerves, and sometimes she snapped at Job for the smallest things—a misplaced tool, a forgotten promise to fetch water.

Job, for his part, was not always patient. The weight of his responsibilities—the lighthouse, Alice, their child to be—rested heavily on him, and when exhaustion set in, he could be short with her. But they never let their tempers linger. At the end of the day, when the light was burning steady and the sea lay dark and endless before them, Job would take Alice's hand, and they would sit in silence, listening to the waves, reminding themselves of the love that had brought them here.

Preparing for Birth

The next few months flashed by, with Alice growing larger by the day. Life on Breaksea continued as normal, with Job tending to the lighthouse and Alice doing her best to prepare for the baby's arrival. But as she neared her due date, they both knew the island was no place for childbirth.

When Alice was a month away from her expected delivery, she caught the store's supply boat back to Albany, where she would wait for the birth in safer conditions. Job had, by then, told her of the acquaintance he had made with William and Eleanor and suggested she seek Eleanor out as a companion while awaiting the baby's arrival.

Eleanor proved to be a great companion, helping Alice where she could and finding a suitable midwife to assist in the birth. And so, on June 30, 1890, Ella Bessie was born, kicking and screaming for attention.

Job arrived the next day with a week's leave and did what he could to help, but as was the way of things, caring for a newborn was primarily a mother's responsibility. Still, he marvelled at the tiny girl in Alice's arms, knowing that life had forever changed once more.

A Year of Stability and Unspoken Thoughts

Another year went by without major upheavals. There was always maintenance work to be done, and often William came over to repair things in the cottage or lighthouse. Twice he brought Eleanor with him, and their visits brought warmth and liveliness to the quiet island.

Sometimes, as Job watched Eleanor move with her usual grace, he found his mind wandering. What if things had turned out differently? What if his life had taken another path? She was still a young and beautiful woman, her laughter light and easy. But then he would turn, and there was Alice—his wife, his partner, the mother of his child—her presence grounding him in the life they had built together. It wasn't a thought he entertained for long, but a man couldn't help but wonder.

Still, life on Breaksea Island continued much as it always had, with its windswept days, its quiet nights, and the steady, unwavering beam of the lighthouse cutting through the darkness. And Job, despite the momentary musings of a life never lived, knew he was exactly where he was meant to be.

And then, just as life in the Symonds household was getting back to normal with Ella Bessie sleeping through the night, Alice again felt the pangs of pregnancy. Another child—another miracle. At thirty-three years old, she had once feared she may never have children, and yet here she was, expecting again. A new life was on the way, and with it, another chapter of their story was about to unfold.

A Second Journey to Albany

The second pregnancy was, as often the case, easier than the first. Either because it truly was, or because Alice was too busy with Ella—now a demanding one-year-old—to dwell on discomfort. Despite her growing belly, life continued as usual. Food needed to be prepared, chores completed, and a wife's duties carried on regardless of how she felt.

As the months passed and Alice gained weight as expected, the time came to think about getting to Albany for the birth. But the supply barge had broken down, and there was no certainty as to when it would arrive. The thought of giving birth on Breaksea Island filled Alice with dread.

One night, as the wind rattled the cottage windows, she turned to Job.
'What if I take the island dinghy and row myself into Albany? I'm strong, Job. I've rowed for hours before. It would at least get me there in time to prepare — and I can stay with Eleanor again.'

Job was reluctant, knowing the dangers of such a trip, but there was no real alternative. He couldn't leave his post at the lighthouse, and someone needed to care for Ella in Alice's absence.
Finally, with great reluctance, he agreed.

The next morning, with the sea relatively calm, Alice boarded the dinghy and set off, rowing the twelve miles across King George Sound at just over eight months pregnant.

From the lantern room high above, Job watched her go — a small figure at the mercy of the wide, glittering sea.
His heart twisted with every dip and rise of the little boat.
If she ran into trouble — if a rogue wave struck or the current dragged her off course — he could do nothing.
No rescue boat. No way to help.

All he could do was send a Morse code message flashing across the bay to the Albany signal station:
'Small boat. Woman aboard. Watch for safe arrival.'
He tapped it out with trembling fingers, staring through the spyglass until he saw the answering blink: **Message received.**

Then he pressed his hand against the cold glass of the lantern window, willing strength into her slender arms, praying she would make it.

Below, the steady rhythm of Alice's oars calmed her nerves. As she made her way across the open water, she noticed something remarkable — a pod of dolphins had appeared, swimming alongside her, their sleek bodies slicing through the waves as if guiding her safely to shore.

Alice smiled, reassured by their presence.
Perhaps they were watching over her.
Perhaps, in some way, the sea was blessing the journey of a mother bringing new life into the world.

Minutes dragged into an hour, an hour dragged into four, the horizon shifting slowly under Job's watchful gaze.
Then, at last, the sharp, bright flashes of Morse light winked back from Albany:
'Arrived safely.'

Job sagged against the railing, his knees weak with relief.
He closed his eyes for a moment, a long, shuddering breath escaping him.
The weight of worry that had gripped him since she set out fell away, leaving only gratitude — deep and wordless — to fill the space where fear had been.

Arrival in Albany and the Birth of Emily Rose

Alice docked the dinghy with a sigh of relief, her arms aching from the long row. A group of fishermen nearby noticed her arrival and hurried over to help, pulling the boat onto higher ground. She offered them a grateful smile before straightening herself, adjusting her shawl, and waddling her way into Albany town as only a heavily pregnant woman could.

Her destination was clear—Eleanor. It was a joy to see her friend again, to share in each other's news and laughter. Eleanor, now the senior housekeeper in the Harbourmaster's home, was thriving, and her lover, William, was making a name for himself in Albany. His craftsmanship was visible in the rising buildings of the town, their stone and timber exteriors standing strong as if they were meant to last a hundred years or more. He was close—so very close—to securing his ticket of leave. Then, at last, he and Eleanor could marry and begin their own family.

Only another two weeks passed before Alice felt the unmistakable signs of labor. The pain began as a dull ache, growing stronger with each passing hour. Eleanor was by her side, as was the midwife they had arranged. The room filled with the tension of childbirth, of whispered encouragements, of hands gripping tightly as waves of pain came and went.

And then, at last, on March 31st, 1892, Emily Rose came into the world, fighting and screaming for attention. Alice, exhausted yet elated, held her daughter close, pressing her lips to the newborn's warm forehead. Another miracle, another blessing.

Alice remained in Albany for four weeks, recovering from the birth and gathering her strength. The time passed in a blur of sleepless nights, tender lullabies, and whispered conversations with Eleanor in the quiet hours. But the island was calling her home, and she knew Job would be waiting, eager to meet his new daughter.

After wrapping Emily Rose tightly against the cool autumn wind, Alice made her way back to the shore. The fishermen who had helped her before were there again, nodding with quiet admiration as she prepared to row back to Breaksea. They helped her launch the dinghy, and with steady strokes, she set off across the water, the infant warm against her chest.

The sea was calm that day, the gentle rhythm of the waves guiding her forward. And as she rowed, she felt a familiar presence in the water—a pod of dolphins, just as before, gliding alongside her, escorting her home.

Job stood waiting on the jetty as she approached, waving eagerly. The moment she set foot on the island again, he was there, wrapping his arms around her, pressing a kiss to her forehead before reaching for the small bundle in her arms.

Alice watched as he gazed down at their new daughter, his face soft with wonder. 'Emily Rose,' she whispered, and he repeated the name with reverence, cradling the tiny girl as though she were the most precious thing in the world.

Alice smiled, knowing that despite all the challenges, all the trials they had faced, their family was growing, and their love remained steadfast. Breaksea Island was home, and here, their story would continue.

Life on Breaksea Continues

And so life on Breaksea continued. The days slipped into routine once more, but now with two little ones to care for, Alice's hands were never idle. Emily Rose grew stronger by the day, and Ella, now full of energy and mischief, found endless ways to keep herself busy—often in ways that left Alice chasing after her.

Job, meanwhile, was getting closer to earning his Harbour Pilot's ticket. His studies continued, and Alice remained his steadfast partner, sending him semaphore questions while he worked in the lighthouse and receiving his Morse code answers in return. It was their own quiet rhythm, a small piece of communication in a place where isolation was a way of life.

Life for a mother with two small children was challenging in any situation, but on an island like Breaksea, it was even more so. There were no neighbours to call on for help, no stores to quickly run to when supplies ran low, no soft grass for children to play on without risk of a rocky fall. Yet, despite the difficulties, Alice found joy in her small family.

Job continued his work, tending to the light, watching the passing ships, ensuring that the waters remained safe for those at sea. Alice carried on with her own duties, caring for the children, preparing meals from their limited supplies, and maintaining their home. There were long days, and sometimes lonely nights when the wind howled through the cottage and she longed for the warmth of a fire in a town surrounded by people. But then she would watch Job with their daughters—lifting Ella onto his shoulders, cradling Emily Rose against his chest—and she knew she was exactly where she was meant to be.

Breaksea had become more than just an island; it was their home, their refuge, and the place where their love, their family, and their future continued to grow.

And grow their family did. It wasn't long before Alice realized she was pregnant again. Her thoughts drifted back to her own family in England, where her mother always seemed to be pregnant, ultimately filling their house with thirteen children.

Mind, her mother had a head start—only seventeen when Alice was born, and forty-one when her last son arrived. It made Alice wonder just how large her own family would become. How would she tell Job when enough was enough?

She still enjoyed the intimacy of their marriage, their quiet moments together when the children were asleep, but she couldn't ignore the reality that one day, there would be a limit. The thought troubled her in ways she hadn't considered before—Job was nine years her junior, and full of vitality. Would he still have energy to spare when she was worn out?

She let the thought linger for a moment before brushing it aside. That was a worry for another day. For now, she was content in their life, their love, and their ever-growing family. Who knew what the future might hold?

Another Birth, Another Bond

And so again, Alice rowed herself into Albany for the birth of their third child in February 1893. The pod of dolphins also met her again and guided her into Albany

Alice was excited to reunite with Eleanor, now married to William, who had secured his ticket of leave . With his strong reputation from his government building work as a prisoner, William's new business as a builder thrived. He was constantly busy, securing more work than he could manage, and together, he and Eleanor had built a solid future.

Now, they had their own cottage, and Eleanor was expecting as well—due around the same time as Alice.

On a fateful Friday, Alice's labour pains began. With the midwife at her side and Eleanor providing support, another daughter, Ellen Annie, was born. The moment was barely settled when fate took a turn—Eleanor clutched her belly, gasping as her own waters broke.

It was a right busy time for the midwife, who barely had a moment to tend to Ellen Annie's cord before rushing to Eleanor's side. Two friends, two mothers, bringing life into the world together.

As they lay together nursing their newborns, Eleanor felt it was time to come clean with Alice and share more of her story—particularly, Job's part in it. She admitted how, in desperation, she had once tried to seduce Job to persuade him to assist in William's escape. How Job, with his steady wisdom, had talked her out of such a reckless plan, making her see the danger it would bring to all involved.

She hesitated before continuing, but Alice listened, calm and understanding. Eleanor admitted they had grown close during that time—perhaps too close—but common sense had ultimately prevailed. The only lapse had been that one kiss on Mount Eliza overlooking Perth, a moment of weakness, yet one that neither had allowed to go any further.

Eleanor turned her gaze to Alice, her voice filled with sincerity. 'I love Job, Alice, but not as a wife loves a husband. I love him as a dear friend, and I will always be grateful for the kindness and strength he gave me in my darkest days. Without him, I might have thrown everything away.'

Alice absorbed the words, watching their daughters sleeping side by side in the nursery. Two little girls, born within a few hours of each other, sharing a bond before they had even opened their eyes to the world. She smiled softly and reached for Eleanor's hand.

'   Do you think they'll remain friends for life'? Alice mused aloud.

Eleanor squeezed her hand in return. 'I hope so. They share so much already. Perhaps fate has intertwined their paths just as it did ours.'

With that, the two mothers rested, their hearts full, their futures forever linked—not just by friendship, but by the children who would grow together, just as they had.

A Journey Home and a New Connection

When Alice rowed herself back out to Breaksea, it was with renewed love for Job and a deeper appreciation of how he had acted when helping Eleanor on the journey to Australia.
Eleanor, having broken her silence on the matter after the birth of their children, had opened up even more during the next four weeks of Alice's recovery.

Their long conversations had strengthened the bond between them, and before Alice left, Eleanor shared some exciting news—
From her position in the Harbourmaster's household, she had overheard the governor telling him plans were in place to lay an undersea telegraph cable to Breaksea Island, connecting it to the wider world.

Alice marvelled at the thought.
Technology had come so far—from the months it took for news to travel by sea to England, now reduced to mere days thanks to the new cable from Darwin to Singapore. A telegraph line to Breaksea would change everything. No longer would they feel so isolated—news, messages, even weather reports could reach them faster than ever before.

She wondered where such rapid advances would lead in the years to come.

As she rowed back across the twelve-mile stretch of water, Alice was once again joined by her pod of dolphins, gracefully gliding alongside her boat as if guiding her home.
It had become a comforting sight; one she had begun to expect on her journeys to and from the mainland.

When she finally arrived at the landing, exhaustion hit her.
The warm summer day had left her hot, sweaty, and short-tempered, but all of that faded

the moment she was greeted by the delighted shrieks of Ella and Emily.
The two little girls ran towards her, eager to meet their new sister, Ellen Annie.

And there was Job, waiting on the dock, his eyes filled with relief and joy.

He hurried down to meet her, reaching out to steady the boat before helping her up onto the boards.
He took Alice's hands, kissed her forehead, and then carefully lifted their newborn daughter from her arms, marvelling at her tiny features.

Alice sighed, letting herself lean against him for a moment, feeling the strength of him — the solidness she'd missed more than she realized.

'I'll tell you this, Job,' she said, wiping her brow, 'that was the last time I row myself across that twelve miles. I've had enough. I'm thirty-three, and I'm passed it.'

Job chuckled, wrapping an arm around her shoulders.

'Then next time, we'll find another way,' he promised.

Alice gave a weary laugh, then tipped her chin up at him.

'And you'll never guess what else I've brought back,' she said, a glint of mischief returning to her eyes.

Job raised an eyebrow, smiling.
'Besides a third daughter and a sunburn?'

She swatted his arm lightly.

'Eleanor heard it straight from the Governor's lips — they're planning to lay a telegraph cable out to Breaksea!'

Job whistled low under his breath, rocking Ellen gently in his arms.

'Proper line, all the way out here?' he said, amazed.
'Blimey... won't be any secrets left then, will there? They'll be sendin' weather reports, messages... maybe even checkin' if we've polished the lantern glass every hour.'

Alice laughed tiredly.

'At least if a storm's coming, we'll have more warning than watching the gulls and hoping for the best.'

Job nodded, his expression turning thoughtful as he looked out across the water.

'World's shrinkin', Alice,' he said quietly. 'Faster than we ever reckoned.'

Alice squeezed his hand.

'And whatever comes,' she said, voice steady, 'we'll face it together.'

And with that, she knew she was truly home.

New Opportunities and a Bold Plan

Another year passed on Breaksea, with life much the same, except now Alice had three daughters to care for. The demands of motherhood filled her days, and while the island remained unchanged, their lives had slowly evolved. Job had now been on Breaksea for six years, rising from Assistant Keeper to Lighthouse Keeper. His career had progressed, and he had passed his exams—he only needed some time ashore to complete his final qualifications.

With the growth of their family and Job's ambitions, they began discussing their options for the next phase of their lives. Opportunities were opening up ashore more frequently now, and with the planned laying of the undersea cable to Breaksea, a unique possibility emerged. They had inside knowledge of the project and, with the right planning, could place a bid for the contract to lay the cable.

William and Eleanor had come out to Breaksea to discuss the cable partnership in detail.
With the work William had been getting, he had managed to save some money, and Job and Alice had been frugal over the years — after all, there had been little to spend money on, as all necessities were provided as part of the lighthouse keeper's role.
Between them, they had built a substantial savings, enough to fund the necessary equipment for the project.

Using their combined resources, they could afford to purchase the barge and the diving equipment required for the cable-laying process.
It was a bold plan, but they had an advantage — no one else had knowledge of the contract yet.
If they moved quickly, Symonds & Jones could lodge a bid before any competition emerged.

The four of them sat around the scarred wooden table in the cottage, teacups scattered among rolls of maps and crumpled sheets of calculations, the air thick with pipe smoke and excitement.

William jabbed a finger at a rough sketch of King George Sound.
'If we set the first anchor point here,' he said, 'it'll give us a straight run to the bay. Easier than tryin' to work around the rocky shallows.'

Job leaned over, frowning thoughtfully.
'Aye, and if we're smart with the tides, we could get the main stretch laid before the storms roll in come spring.'

Alice, brushing a stray curl behind her ear, smiled as she poured more tea.
'Sounds as though you two have half the work done already. Pity you can't just tell the sea what to do.'

William gave a bark of laughter.
'Tell the sea what to do? Hah! Next, you'll be suggestin' we teach the fish to haul the cable for us.'

Eleanor chuckled softly, smoothing the hem of her dress.
'At least you'd have a workforce that doesn't argue back.'

They laughed, the easy camaraderie filling the small room.

After a moment, Eleanor leaned closer.
'Oh — you'll never guess the news from town. Old Mr. Wainwright's bull broke loose again — charged clean through the hotel garden. You should've seen the innkeeper chasing it with a broom, swearing fit to raise the dead.'

William shook his head, grinning.
'Bet the old fool blamed the council roads somehow.'

Alice laughed, her eyes bright.
'Poor Mr. Wainwright. That bull's got more sense than he does.'

Job sat back, letting the warmth of the moment settle over him.
Friends, plans, laughter — the island felt less lonely tonight.

But beneath the merriment, the future was quietly assembling itself.
This was more than just a business venture — it was a chance to shape their own destiny, to create something lasting.

Job and Alice exchanged a glance across the table — a small, steady look full of understanding.

Their time on Breaksea was drawing to a close.
A new chapter awaited, rising over the horizon like the tide, and it was one they were ready to embrace.

A New Path Ashore

William and Job worked tirelessly to finalize the cable-laying contract. Every detail was scrutinised—cost estimates, manpower, the logistics of transporting the cable, and the methods they would use to anchor it securely along the ocean floor. When the final document was prepared, they submitted it to the Harbour Master.

The Harbour Master, a shrewd but fair man, raised an eyebrow as he read through the proposal. How had these two known about the project before it had even been formally announced? Then, realization dawned—of course, they would have heard whispers of it through their lighthouse duties and connections with the maritime industry.

He was impressed. Their initiative was undeniable, and the price they had quoted was both competitive and reasonable. With a knowing nod, he rubber-stamped the tender and forwarded it to Perth with a strong recommendation for approval.

He also knew that Job's time as a lighthouse keeper was nearing its end. Job had ambitions beyond Breaksea, and he was only a short time away from completing his pilot's ticket. The Harbour Master had a young assistant keeper at Point King Lighthouse eager for a promotion, and an idea formed in his mind.

When the next supply tender made its way to Breaksea, it carried a message for Job — an offer for the position of Harbour Signal Man.
The role required precision and knowledge of maritime navigation, making it an ideal stepping stone towards his eventual goal of becoming a pilot.
It would also provide stability while the cable-laying contract was being processed, which could take up to a year before work commenced.

When Job received the message, he found Alice sitting on the bench outside the cottage, darning a pair of tiny stockings.

He waved the letter aloft.
'Got a notion to make us town folk,' he said, grinning.

Alice looked up, shielding her eyes against the morning sun.
'Town folk? What are you talking about?'

He handed her the message, watching her read.
As her eyes moved down the page, a slow smile spread across her face.

'Oh, Job,' she said softly. 'A real house. Shops. Neighbours who aren't just seagulls and shearwaters.'

He chuckled, sitting down beside her.
'And no more boilin' muttonbird eggs till the smell knocks ye sox off.'

Alice gave a mock shudder.
'I'll not miss those one bit. Nor having to ration out the flour and sugar as if I'm guarding a treasure chest.'

Job leaned back, looking out over the restless sea.
'I reckon we'll miss this old rock, though,' he said. 'In its own rough way.'

Alice nodded, her fingers still resting lightly on the letter.
'We made a life here. Had our girls here. Learned we could face whatever came.'

He looked at her; at the salty breeze lifting strands of her hair.
'You sure you're ready for town life, Mrs. Symonds? All them fine ladies and tea parties?'

She laughed, a bright, clear sound.
'If it means fresh bread and a decent roast now and then, I'll learn to curtsey if I must.'

Job reached for her hand, rough palm to soft fingers.

'Then it's settled,' he said.

They both knew the truth of it deep down: Breaksea had forged them — tested them, hardened them — but it was time to move on.

Alice gave a small, thoughtful smile.
'Think they'll let you keep your rough old boots in town, or will they make you wear shiny shoes?'

Job laughed.
'I'll wear shiny boots if it gets us off this rock with all our teeth intact.'

Later, as they packed up their belongings, Alice stood by the cottage door, watching the familiar waves crash against the shore. Their daughters played nearby, oblivious to the change about to take place in their lives.

The lighthouse had been their home, a place of solitude and endurance, but a new future awaited them on the mainland.

With a deep breath, she turned to Job.
'Are you ready?'

He smiled, placing a reassuring hand on her shoulder.
'More than ready.'

And with that, the Symonds family prepared to embark on their next chapter — one filled with new opportunities, fresh challenges, and a world beyond the confines of Breaksea Island.

The day had come. After six years of isolation on Breaksea Island, Job, Alice, and their children were finally leaving their lighthouse home for a new life in Albany. The move brought a mix of excitement and nostalgia. Alice, while eager for the conveniences of town life, couldn't help feeling a pang of sadness as she looked around their small cottage one last time. This had been their home, where their family had grown, where they had endured storms and celebrated new life. But the time for change had arrived.

The supply boat arrived early, and Job oversaw the loading of their few belongings. The lighthouse, which had been his world for so long, now stood as a silent sentinel behind him. Alice gathered the children, ensuring that Ella, Emily Rose, and little Ellen Annie were secure before stepping onto the boat. As they pushed away from the jetty, she watched the island grow smaller, the beam of the lighthouse a distant flicker against the sky.

Arriving in Albany felt like stepping into another world. The town was alive with the sounds of horses' hooves clattering on the streets, merchants calling from their shops, and the distant chime of ship bells from the bustling port. The contrast from Breaksea's solitude was almost overwhelming. Alice marvelled at the sight of people moving in all directions, the lined storefronts filled with goods she had long gone without, and the undeniable energy of a growing town.

Their new home, a modest but comfortable cottage near the harbor, was a luxury compared to the sparse accommodations of the island. The children were thrilled to have more space to explore, and Alice took great joy in knowing she could now buy fresh produce, new clothes, and household necessities without waiting weeks for a supply boat.

For Job, taking on his new role as the Harbour Signalman was both an adjustment and an opportunity. His days were now spent overseeing the comings and goings of ships, ensuring smooth communication between the vessels and the town. It was a far cry from the solitude of the lighthouse, but he welcomed the challenge, knowing it was another step towards his ultimate goal—earning his pilot's licence and securing a future for his family on the mainland.

Alice quickly adapted to town life, reconnecting with Eleanor and embracing the newfound ability to socialise beyond the occasional supply boat visit. The simple act of visiting a market, chatting with neighbours, and walking along Albany's streets made her feel a part of something larger than the vast isolation of Breaksea had ever allowed.

As the weeks passed, the Symonds family settled into their new routine. Life in Albany was different, bustling, and filled with opportunities. Though they had left the

lighthouse behind, they carried with them the strength and resilience forged on Breaksea. With new prospects ahead and the cable-laying contract still pending, Job and Alice knew that their adventure was far from over. A new chapter had begun, and with it, the promise of a future shaped by their own hands.

Alice and Eleanor now met regularly for tea, their children playing together while they chatted about their families and the town's latest news. Ellen Annie and Eleanor's daughter, Bridget, had become inseparable, always dashing about together, giggling and getting into mischief. Meanwhile, the older Symonds girls delighted in helping care for Eleanor's newest addition, baby Jacob, just a few months old.

One afternoon, as they sat in Eleanor's parlor with their cups of tea, watching the children play, Eleanor tilted her head and gave Alice a knowing smile. 'So, when are you going to tell Job?'

Alice nearly choked on her tea. 'Tell him what'?

Eleanor chuckled. 'That you're expecting again. I can see it in your face.'

Alice's eyes widened in shock. 'How did you know? '

Eleanor reached over and patted her hand. 'I've had two of my own now—I know the signs.'

Alice exhaled and laughed softly, shaking her head. 'I suppose I should tell him soon.'

As the two women shared a moment of understanding, Alice realized how much had changed in her life. Gone were the days of isolation, of relying only on Job and herself. She had friends, a community, and a new future unfolding before her. And with another child on the way, life in Albany was about to become even more exciting.

A Son at Last

In October 1895, the Symonds family welcomed their first son. The arrival of a boy ,
his name chosen years before was Henry Homer after his grandfather brought a
renewed sense of excitement and joy, not just for Alice but especially for Job. As much
as he adored his daughters, having a son was a moment of great pride—something as a
husband and a father he had looked forward to since Alice arrived. He was beaming
when he first held the tiny infant in his arms, his grip gentle yet strong as he whispered,
'My boy.'

This time, the transition into caring for a newborn was smoother for Alice. Unlike in
Breaksea, where she had to manage everything with little outside help, she now had an
expanding group of friends who were ready to assist. Many of them were also friends of
Eleanor, forming a strong support network that helped her navigate the first weeks with
a newborn.

While Alice focused on her son, the older Symonds girls eagerly helped care for baby
Jacob at Eleanor's home. Ellen Annie and Bridget, as always, were inseparable, running
through the house and playing as if they had been sisters since birth.

Alice, sipping tea one afternoon with Eleanor while their children played, sighed with
relief. 'I don't know how I managed before, doing this all alone on Breaksea.'

Eleanor laughed. 'You didn't have much choice then, did you? But now, you've got
us. And we'll make sure you have all the help you need.'

Alice smiled warmly, looking at her son in her arms. This time, everything was
different. This time, she wasn't alone.

Another Surprise

Life had become much easier since settling into Albany.
There were more hands to help, more luxuries at her fingertips, and far fewer hardships
than life on Breaksea had offered.
Alice finally felt she had some control over her days, rather than constantly battling the
elements, supplies, and isolation.

But as much as life had settled, some things remained constant — one of them being
Job's affections.

Within a month of Henry's arrival, Job had started looking at her with that
familiar twinkle in his eye, the same one that had always preceded his amorous advances.
In the past, she had been more hesitant after childbirth, preferring to give herself ample
time to recover.
But this time, she felt different. Relaxed. Comfortable.

She had missed the quiet intimacy they shared, the small moments of closeness between the chaos of raising a growing family.
And so, when Job reached for her, she didn't resist.

Weeks passed, and Alice went about her daily routines, tending to the children, visiting Eleanor, and managing the household.
But something nagged at her — a realisation creeping in slowly.
Her monthly cycle had not returned.

Trying to push the worry aside, she wondered nervously — could she now be infertile? Had childbirth changed her in some way?

She made an appointment with the town doctor, hoping for reassurance.
But as soon as he examined her, his response was immediate.

'Alice,' he said with a knowing smile, 'I do believe you may be pregnant again.'

Shock washed over her.
Pregnant? Again?
But Henry was still so small — there would only be ten months between them!

She left the doctor's office in a daze, her hands protectively resting over her stomach.

How would she tell Job?
More importantly, how would she manage two babies under a year apart?

As she walked back towards home, she let out a long breath.
Ready or not, it seemed another little Symonds was on the way.

That evening, after the supper dishes were washed and the children settled, Alice found Job in the backyard, tinkering with an old fishing reel.
He looked up at her approach, his face breaking into an easy smile.

'You're back early, love. Doctor sort you out?' he asked, wiping his hands on a rag.

Alice hesitated, twisting her apron strings between her fingers.

'Sort of,' she said slowly.

Job straightened, sensing something more behind her words.
He crossed the yard in three long strides and laid a gentle hand on her arm.

'What is it, Alice? You're not unwell, are you?'

She shook her head quickly, blinking back sudden tears she hadn't realized were gathering.
'No, not unwell. Just... surprised.'

He frowned, tilting his head. 'Surprised?'

Alice turned, ladle in hand, and with a mischievous twinkle in her eye, dropped a bombshell. 'Well, Job darling, it won't be long before another joins this gang of Symonds.'

Job chuckled, shaking his head. 'Naa, that won't happen for a while yet.'

Alice smirked. 'Don't be too sure, Job. The doctor told me this morning—I'm pregnant again.'

Job froze mid-motion, his smile faltering. 'But… how can that be'?

'But Henry's barely out o' his swaddlin' clothes!'

'I know,' she said, half laughing, half crying. 'There'll be only ten months between them!'

Job rubbed the back of his neck, a slow grin spreading across his face.

'Well,' he said, 'I always did say we were good at workin' together.'

Alice thumped him lightly on the chest, laughing properly now despite herself.

'You great oaf,' she said, though the affection in her voice was clear.
'What are we going to do with two babes under a year old?'

Job pulled her into his arms without hesitation.
'Same thing we've always done,' he murmured into her hair.
'Face it together.'

Job stared at her, his expression a mix of astonishment and amusement. 'But… they'll only be ten months apart!'

Alice laughed, placing a comforting hand on his shoulder. 'Yes, my bright one, they will.'

For a moment, Job was speechless. Then, he exhaled a deep breath, shaking his head as a slow grin spread across his face. 'Well, I suppose we're in for another adventure.'

Alice chuckled. 'That we are, Job. That we are.'

As the children ran around them, completely oblivious to the revelation, Job leaned in and kissed Alice's forehead. 'I wouldn't want it any other way.'

And with that, the Symonds family prepared to grow once more, their journey in Albany becoming even richer than they had ever imagined.

Meanwhile, Job and William were nearing the start of their cable-laying enterprise. The long-awaited cable had arrived in Albany, and preparations were well underway. Job and William had begun building the support structures at each end—one on Breaksea Island and the other on the mainland—ready to anchor the cable as it came ashore. The excitement of the project gave Job renewed energy, knowing that it would not only be a significant step in Albany's development but also a lucrative and stable business venture for their families.

Despite his demanding work, Job never failed to cherish the moments he had at home. Each evening, he returned to a lively household filled with the laughter and chatter of four children ranging from three months to five years old. As soon as he stepped through the door, the older girls rushed to greet him, wrapping their arms around his legs, while Alice, balancing the routine of home life, handed him young Henry so she could finish preparing the evening meal.

Job, as tired as he was, loved every bit of it. He lifted Henry high into the air, making the baby squeal with delight, then sat down with the girls, listening to their stories of the day. The sight of his growing family filled him with immense pride. As he looked over at Alice, her apron dusted with flour, her cheeks rosy from the warmth of the stove, he grinned and said, 'This is wonderful. Here we are, with a complete family, and now a son. What could be better than this'?

By now Job and William had begun the cable-laying enterprise in earnest. The long-awaited cable had arrived in Albany, and work commenced immediately. As the massive coil of cable was carefully transported to the staging area, the two men oversaw every step, ensuring that the operation went smoothly. They had employed a diver to guide the cable along the seabed, securing it with the anchors that William had designed and constructed. Each day brought progress, and within two months, the cable was fully laid, stretching between Breaksea Island and the mainland.

The work, however, was far from over. Experts were brought in to make the final connections, linking the cable into the vast network that now extended across Australia and beyond. From Breaksea, the telegraph line reached Darwin, branching down the east coast to Sydney and across the sea to Singapore, connecting through Asia and Europe all the way to London. It was a marvel of modern technology, a feat that only years ago would have seemed impossible.

Alice marvelled at the sheer advancement of it all. She thought back to the days when letters took months to reach England, carried by ship through treacherous seas. Now, with a few clicks of a telegraph key, a message could cross the world in mere days. 'Isn't technology marvellous?' she mused to Eleanor as they sipped tea one afternoon, watching their children play in the garden.

With the contract successfully completed, Job and William turned their attention to what came next. They sold off the equipment they had purchased for the project, the barge, the diving gear, and other specialized tools. The contract fee, combined with the sale of assets, left both families in a position neither could have ever imagined when they first arrived in Australia.

One evening, with the hard work behind them, Job and William sat on the veranda of William's home, sharing a well-earned beer. Their wives sat nearby, chatting while the children played, laughter echoing through the warm Albany night.

William took a deep swig of his drink and looked at Job with a grin. 'We're damn lucky, you know.'

Job chuckled. 'Aye, we are. Who would have thought it? Two blokes thrown together by chance, now with family, money in the bank, and a future ahead of us.'

Eleanor smiled, glancing at Alice. 'And to think, it all started with a foolish idea of mine. If I had carried on with my ridiculous plan to break William out, who knows where we'd be now? Probably halfway across the country, hiding like criminals. Or dangling on a rope more likely'

Alice reached over and squeezed her friend's hand. 'But you didn't. You made the right choice. And look at us now—all of us together, building a life.'

Job laughed and raised his bottle. 'To fate, then. And to whatever comes next.'

As the glasses clinked together, the two families sat in contentment, knowing that, despite all the twists and turns, they had ended up exactly where they were meant to be.

A Growing Family and New Horizons

With the cable-laying project complete and financial security within their grasp, life in Albany settled into a comfortable rhythm. Job continued working in the harbor, joining the pilot crew as he set his sights on earning his full Harbour Pilot's license. The work was demanding but rewarding, bringing him closer to his goal of navigating the waters as an expert mariner.

In October 1896, Alice gave birth to their second son, Joseph. The household, already bustling with energy, grew even livelier with the arrival of another baby. Alice was grateful to have help from her growing circle of friends, especially Eleanor, who always seemed to know when she needed an extra hand. As Joseph grew, so did the family's sense of belonging in Albany.

Three years later, in 1899, another daughter, Eva, was born. By now, Alice had fully embraced the joys and chaos of motherhood in a house filled with young children. The days were long but fulfilling, and with each new arrival, she and Job found their bond strengthening.

Job's work in Albany continued, and by the turn of the century, his diligence had paid off. In January 1901, he was officially appointed as a Harbour Pilot on Rottnest Island, a role that came with great responsibility and prestige. When Alice heard of the offer, she gasped. 'What? Not another island?'

The thought of returning to an isolated life unsettled her, but Job quickly comforted her. 'This one is different, Alice. There's a community, and even a prison for native prisoners. We won't be alone like we were on Breaksea.'

The decision to leave Albany was not made lightly.
It wasn't just about moving to another island — it meant leaving behind the close-knit friendships they had built over the years.
Ellen and Bridget, now eight years old, had remained the closest of friends, inseparable since their infancy.

The thought of separating them was difficult for both Alice and Eleanor, who had become like sisters over the years.
William, now a free man and a successful builder, had established himself well in Albany, but the idea of being apart from the Symonds family weighed on him too.

They all gathered one last evening at the Symonds' modest cottage, the children sprawled on the rug playing, the adults nursing cups of strong tea laced with a drop of rum to soften the mood.

William leaned back in his chair, hands behind his head, surveying Job with a grin.

'Well, Captain Symonds,' he said, his voice teasing, 'off to rule over another rock, are ye?'

Job chuckled, running a hand through his hair.
'Not quite a kingdom, mate — just another post. But the pay's good, and the lighthouse comes with a roof that doesn't leak in every storm.'

Alice laughed softly.
'And a kitchen that's bigger than a cupboard, which I consider a victory.'

Eleanor leaned forward, eyes shining with a mix of pride and sadness.
'You'll be missed, Alice. There won't be a day I boil the kettle without thinking, 'I wonder what she's doing just now.'

Alice smiled warmly.
'I'll be thinking the same — and sending letters faster than you can bake a loaf.'

William shook his head, pretending to sigh.
'All these ladies and their letters. Me, I'll be lucky if Job scrawls two words by Christmas.'

Job laughed.
'You'll get two words — if you're lucky. 'Still alive.' That'll do, won't it?'

They all laughed, but the sound was threaded with sadness.

'Perhaps one day,' William said, his voice turning thoughtful, 'we'll move closer to you. With my work expanding, there's no telling where we'll end up.'

Eleanor nodded, her eyes misty as she glanced at Bridget and Ellen, their heads bent close together in shared secrets.
'And with the way these two girls carry on, I don't think they'd let us stay apart for long.'

The words gave Alice a small measure of comfort as they packed up their belongings and prepared for their next chapter.

Leaving Albany was bittersweet, but the hope of a future reunion with the Jones family softened the farewell.

Later that year, Rottnest Island welcomed its newest resident.
In the peaceful isolation of their new home, Alice gave birth to their daughter, Victoria, who became known as Queenie.
As she cradled her newborn in her arms, looking out across the island's vast blue horizon, she reflected on the incredible journey that had brought them here.

From the harsh winds of Breaksea, to the bustling town of Albany, and now to the remote beauty of Rottnest, their lives had taken them places they could never have imagined.
But no matter where they were, one thing remained constant — the love and strength of their growing family.

The morning of their departure was bright and sharp, the sky a hard blue over   the harbour.

The Symonds family stood on the jetty, their few trunks already loaded onto the small steamer that would carry them across the water to Fremantle and then onwards to Rottnest.

Eleanor held Alice's hands tightly, neither of them speaking at first.
The words felt too heavy, too tangled.

Finally, Eleanor whispered, 'Write often. Tell me everything — even the silly things.'

Alice smiled through the prickle of tears.
'I will. And you — kiss Bridget for me when she's missing Ellen.'

The two women hugged fiercely; the kind of hug that tried to stitch the distance closed before it even opened.

Nearby, William clapped Job on the back — a hearty, rough thud that lingered a moment longer than usual.

'Take care of her, mate,' William said gruffly.
'And yourself.'

Job gave a lopsided smile.
'Always do.'

The children waved wildly — Ellen blowing kisses, Bridget hopping from foot to foot, both trying to outdo each other in farewell.

As the steamer's whistle sounded its low, mournful note, Job guided Alice and the children up the gangplank.
At the top, he turned for one last look — at the friends who had become family, the town that had been their safe harbour, the life they were leaving behind.

William raised a hand in a salute.
Eleanor wiped at her eyes with the corner of her apron.
And the wind carried their shouted goodbyes across the water long after the little ship had pulled away.

Life Begins on Rottnest 1901

The boat nudged against the Rottnest jetty, and Alice stepped ashore, The brilliant white sand stretched away in all directions, dazzling under the morning sun, and the sea shimmered a clear, endless blue — a wild, beautiful canvas for the next chapter of their lives.

Job lifted the luggage with an easy grin, the girls already skipping ahead up the path towards the cluster of weathered cottages. They hadn't gone far up the sandy track when Ellen suddenly gasped, pointing excitedly at a clump of low bushes near the path.

'Look! What's that?'

Alice turned just in time to see a small, round creature hop into view — bright-eyed, with soft brown fur, twitching whiskers, and a gentle, curious expression.

'It's a quokka,' Job said, smiling as he crouched down beside the girls. 'Only place in the world you'll find 'em is here.'

The creature stood upright on its hind legs, nose twitching at the new arrivals. And nestled snugly in its pouch, a tiny pink face peeked out — a baby, barely bigger than a thumb.

Bridget clapped her hands in delight. 'It's got a baby! Look, Ellen, it's got a little one "

Ellen knelt in the sand, giggling softly as the quokka hopped a step closer, apparently unafraid.

Henry, never one to be left out, waddled over on unsteady legs, arms flapping with excitement. The quokka twitched its ears, gave a soft chattering sound, and to everyone's amazement, stayed right where it was.

'It's welcoming us,' Ellen whispered, her eyes wide with wonder.

Alice watched them — the girls' faces shining with delight, Henry squealing with laughter, Job crouched nearby with a grin — and felt her heart swell.

This island, with its scrubby trees and endless sky, its white beaches and strange, smiling creatures, was not just a place to live.

It was their new home

The Symonds children about 1900

Rottnest Island was unlike any place the Symonds family had lived before. It was not as isolated as Breaksea, nor as bustling as Albany, but rather a world of its own—a strange blend of serenity and hardship, beauty and restraint. For Job, it was a step forwards in his maritime career, guiding ships safely into Fremantle. For Alice, it was another adjustment, another test of resilience, but at least this time, she was not alone.

The island's landscape was rugged and wind-swept, with the unmistakable scent of salt and kelp carried by the ever-present breeze. The quokkas darted about like mischievous spirits, always underfoot, and the prison at the heart of the island cast a long shadow over daily life. The native prisoners, their presence an open secret, toiled under the watchful eyes of their uniformed guards. Some of their wives, like Milly and Anna, worked in the homes of the island's residents, including the Symonds'. They helped Alice with the washing up before returning to the makeshift camps near the gaol, where their husbands were held.

Despite the grim realities of the prison, life for the children on Rottnest was filled with adventure. School was held in the old salt store, its high windows letting in slanted beams of golden light as the teacher guided them through lessons. It was said that the ghost of a prisoner, suffocated by falling salt bags, haunted the place. Ella Bessie and Ellen had delighted in scaring young Joe and Eva with tales of the ghost's mournful wails, making them dread the day they'd have to attend school.

One evening, as Job and Alice sat on their veranda, watching the children chase quokkas in the twilight, Job stretched out his legs and said, 'Alice, can you believe it? Australia is one nation now. Just a few years ago, we were a colony, and now we're part of the Commonwealth.'

Alice smiled, setting down her mending. 'Yes, I read about it in the paper. Federation, they're calling it. Western Australia was the last to join, wasn't it'?

"It was," Job said. "But now we're joined up with the other states. They had a big parade in Perth for Commonwealth Day. One of the pilots told me thousands turned out. They even gave the kids free rides on the trams. Imagine that—trams!"

Alice laughed. "Try that here on Rottnest. The quokkas would be all over the tracks."

Job grinned. 'And in March, they held the first election for the new government, remember, I went into Fremantle to vote. Felt strange, seeing all the people lined up, knowing we were picking men for all Australia, not just here.'

Alice's smile faded. 'I read they've brought in that White Australia law. Means anyone who isn't European can't come in.'

Job sighed, rubbing his chin. 'It's a complicated thing. On one hand, they don't want cheap labour driving wages down. But on the other…' He gestured towards the camp where the native prisoners and their families stayed. 'Not everyone gets a fair say in these things, do they?'Alice nodded but remained silent. Some things, she felt, were too large to change.

The conversation shifted as Job recalled a name from Alice's past. 'Speaking of change, did you see that the Kalgoorlie Pipeline is nearly done? C.Y. O'Connor's project. Didn't you work for his family once?'

Alice nodded. 'Yes, I was a governess for his children. He was a kind man, brilliant, but somehow different. People said he was mad for trying to bring water to the goldfields but look at it now. Kalgoorlie is growing because of his vision.'

'A shame he didn't live to see it finished,' Job said quietly.

Alice sighed, remembering the tragic news of O'Connor's suicide. 'Some people don't realize the weight a great mind carries. But his work lives on.'

One of Job's greatest challenges on Rottnest came on a stormy night when the Norwegian barque *Waimea* found herself in dire straits.
With the wind howling and waves crashing against the reefs, the ship had missed its chance to sail safely into Gage Roads.
Job and his crew, caught unprepared, were having a drink at the public house, warming their bones after a long day's watch, the fire crackling low in the hearth and a battered deck of cards scattered across the table.

The door slammed open with a bang loud enough to silence the room.
The lookout's mate stumbled inside, rain dripping from his oilskin coat, face flushed with urgency.

'Waimea's missed the mark!' he shouted. 'She's in the breakers — she's goin' to ground if we don't move!'

For a split second, the tavern froze — mugs half-raised, cards half-played.
Then the room erupted into action.

'Blast it all!' Job was already on his feet, knocking over his stool.
'Get the men! Oars to the ready!'

'She'll be smashed ta kindling if we don't reach her!' one of the oarsmen yelled, grabbing his cap and bolting for the door.

Another voice from the corner barked, 'Which reef? North side or South?'

'South Passage!' the lookout's mate cried, gasping for breath. 'She's driftin' fast!'

Never been done before they shouted from the bar, not at night during a storm, that South Passage is a grave yard.

Job grabbed his jacket, shouting over the rising wind that now howled through the open doorway.
'Double crews! We'll need every hand pullin' tonight!'

Boots pounded across the wooden floorboards as the pilots and oarsmen rushed into the storm, wrestling their gear into place.
The air outside was thick with salt spray and flying sand, the night black as pitch.

They battled their way down to the boat, muscles straining against the roaring wind, every man knowing how slim the chances were — but not one hesitating.

Later, Job would recall that it was the finest display of teamwork he had ever witnessed, as the crew pulled against the furious current, every stroke wringing the strength from their arms.

They had one chance to put Job aboard the vessel, and they did so in the nick of time — the small pilot boat rising and falling like a leaf on the monstrous waves as Job leapt across the gap.

Guided only by his deep knowledge of the unmarked reefs, his hands steady on the wheel, his eyes searching through the rain, Job navigated the *Waimea* through the South Passage — a narrow, treacherous cut in the reef, hardly wider than the ship in places.

Hard enough in daylight — near madness at night, in a storm.

But Job, mustering every ounce of skill and instinct he possessed, led the crippled vessel through to safety.

The next morning, the newspapers praised his daring seamanship, calling it nothing short of miraculous.

And in the weeks that followed, the Governor of Western Australia Sir Arthur Lawley personally presented him with a diamond scarf pin in recognition of his bravery and exceptional service.

The morning was clear and crisp, with the scent of salt and eucalyptus heavy in the air.
At the front steps of the Fremantle Civic Hall, a small crowd had gathered — officials in dark coats, ladies in bright summer dresses, a handful of rougher hands from the docks, and Job's own crew standing stiffly in borrowed jackets.

Job shifted uneasily on the polished floorboards, tugging at the unfamiliar stiffness of his collar.
He would have felt more comfortable hauling on an oar or standing a wheel in a storm — not being the centre of attention like this.

At the front of the hall, Sir Arthur Lawley, Governor of Western Australia, stepped forward, the diamond pin glinting in the morning light as he held it between thumb and forefinger.

The Governor smiled warmly.

'Mr. Symonds,' he said, his voice carrying easily across the hall, 'it gives me great pleasure to recognize your exceptional service and courage.'

Job swallowed, inclined his head respectfully.

Sir Arthur continued,
'Guiding the *Waimea* to safety through the South Passage, at night, in a storm, where many would not have dared — it was an act of extraordinary seamanship and nerve.'

There was a smattering of applause from the crowd — polite at first, then swelling as the dockworkers and pilots banged their hands together with real enthusiasm.

Sir Arthur beckoned Job forward, and pinned the sparkling diamond scarf pin to the lapel of his jacket, stepping back to offer his hand.

Job grasped it firmly, clearing his throat.

'Thank ye kindly, Your Excellency,' Job said, his voice rough with emotion but steady.
'I'm proud to accept it — but I'd not be standin' here if it weren't for the lads that got me aboard that night.'

He turned slightly, nodding towards the cluster of pilots and oarsmen at the back of the room.

'Best crew a man could hope for — pulled like devils against a sea fit to tear the world in two. I owe 'em more than I can say.'

A ripple of laughter and a few proud cheers rose from his men.

Sir Arthur smiled even wider, clearly pleased by Job's humility.

'It speaks well of a man, Mr. Symonds, when he remembers those who stand beside him in the storm,' he said warmly.
'You have done your colony proud — and you have honoured your mates in doing so.'

He paused, glancing thoughtfully at the crowd.

'Western Australia could do with a few more like you.'

Job flushed, murmured a quiet, 'Thank you, sir,' and stepped back, feeling the reassuring weight of the pin on his chest and the heavier, steadier weight of the pride in his heart.

He caught the eye of one of his crew — a wink, a grin — and the unspoken bond between them all was stronger than any glittering prize.

Later that afternoon, the polished speeches and formalities behind them, Job and his crew found themselves crowded into the snug back room of McTavish's Public House, the old floorboards creaking under the weight of wet boots and good spirits.

Job leaned on the bar, the diamond pin still gleaming awkwardly on his jacket like a lighthouse beacon.
He tugged at it self-consciously, grumbling,
'Feels heavier than a good anchor chain, this does.'

A roar of laughter went up from the men.

'Better watch yerself, Job!' one of the oarsmen hollered.
'Flashin' that thing around, ye'll have every magpie from Fremantle to Perth tryin' to nick it off ye!'

Another man thumped his pint onto the table.
'Should've pinned it to his hat — that way we'd all see him comin' and get out the road!'

Job raised his glass with a crooked grin.
'Aye, give me a gale and a broken tiller any day over standin' still while some fine gent sticks pins in me like a prize goose.'

The men howled with laughter, a few slapping the table so hard their ales sloshed over the sides.

One of the younger crewmen piped up cheekily,
'What's next, Job? Goin' to start givin' navigation lessons to the Governor's butler?'

Job snorted, taking a long pull from his glass.

'Nay, lad. I'll leave teachin' to folk with softer heads than me.'
He raised an eyebrow.
'Though if I catch any of ye lot callin' me *Sir Job* even once, I'll have ye scrubbing barnacles off me dinghy 'til Christmas.'

More laughter, louder this time — but behind the teasing, the men's faces shone with pride.

They knew what Job had done that night.
They knew he'd earned every scrap of the honour he'd been given — and more.

As the sun sank low outside and the oil lamps lit up the smoky room, Job clinked his glass against the nearest pint.

'To the crew that pulled me through,' he said simply.

The men raised their mugs high, and for a moment — just a breath of time between laughter and song — there was nothing but loyalty, pride, and the steady, unspoken bond of men who had faced death together and come through smiling.

In 1903, a bubonic plague scare in Fremantle had many concerned. One day, Alice came home from the market with a worried look.

'Job, they say there's plague in the port towns again. Ships are being held offshore, and the authorities are inspecting every vessel.'

Job frowned. 'I'll have to be careful when piloting ships in. If it reaches Bunbury, the whole town will be in a panic.'

Alice kept the children close for the next few weeks, and eventually, the danger passed. But it was another reminder of how quickly things could change in this young nation.

By this time, change was inevitable. The long-promised pilot steamer finally arrived, and with it, the relocation of pilots to Fremantle. The Symonds family was the last to leave Rottnest, remaining for another six months before their final departure. Job had already been preparing for this transition, and when the position of Assistant Harbour Master in Bunbury was advertised, he seized the opportunity.

But there was another twist of fate in store—William and Eleanor were moving to Bunbury as well. William's construction business had flourished, and with building work booming in Bunbury, it made sense to relocate. He still had teams in Albany and Perth, but Bunbury was fast becoming a major centre of development.

For Alice and Eleanor, it will be a joyous reunion. They had written regularly faithfully recanting their news , but nothing compared to being near each other again. For Ellen and Bridget, now ten years old, it will be the fulfillment of a long-awaited dream. They had spent years growing up together and needed each other more than ever as they approached the cusp of adolescence.

As the ferry bound for Fremantle carried them away from Rottnest, the children clutched their belongings, waving at the receding shoreline. Alice stood beside Job, exhaling a long breath. 'At least Bunbury isn't another island.'

Job chuckled, wrapping an arm around her shoulders. 'No, love, it's not. But it's another beginning.'

The sea had shaped their lives, carried them to new places, and tested their resilience time and time again. Now, as they prepared to step onto the mainland once more, the Symonds family braced for their next adventure—this time, in Bunbury.

Shifting Sands and Whispered Promises (1904–1915)

The sound of gulls echoed through the salty breeze as Job tightened the latch on the small cottage gate. Bunbury, now a growing port town with the scent of opportunity on every corner, had welcomed Job, Alice, and the children with open arms—or at least with the offer of a modest worker's cottage provided by the Port Authority.

Their long-standing friendship with William and Eleanor had only deepened since both families had moved closer. Their houses were a short walk apart, and it became a weekly tradition for the men to share a drink and chew over the headlines at the local pub, while Alice and Eleanor swapped gossip and homemade scones over endless cups of tea.

One Thursday evening, Job and William sat on wooden stools outside the back door, each nursing a cold beer. The air was thick with the scent of eucalyptus and salt spray.

'You seen the *Kalgoorlie Miner* today?' William asked, handing over a folded paper. 'They reckon the rail link from Perth to Kal is going ahead. Big news.'

Job nodded, scanning the front page. 'Federation's makin' waves, mate. We're not just colonies anymore. Still, you ask some folks, they think all the power's gone east.'

William laughed. 'That's politics for you. But I'll say this—business is booming. I've got crews working on government housing now. None of that flimsy stuff, mind you. Solid builds. Proper homes.'

He leaned back, taking a long swig from his bottle before adding, 'You catch that other story—about the Bonneville mine?'

Job shook his head. 'No, what's happened now?'

William's face lit with the thrill of a good yarn. 'Flooded shaft. Whole lower levels went under. Poor sod, Charlie Vanzetti, got trapped down there. Thought he was done for.'

Job whistled low. 'Christ. How'd they get him out?'

William grinned. 'Diving suit, our old one from Albany, rig. Helmet, hose, boots— the lot.'

Job let out a bark of laughter. 'No bloody way! Like the same one we used out to Breaksea?'

'Exactly ,' William said, tapping his bottle against Job's in a mock toast. 'Some smart fella reckoned it was the only chance. Lowered a diver down through the flooded tunnels. Took days, first getting a light and some tucker to him , but they hauled young Charlie out, alive as you please.'

Job shook his head, a slow smile spreading across his face. 'Funny how things turn out, eh? We sweated and cussed getting that cable laid—and now the same gear's savin' miners halfway across the country.'

'Aye,' William said, his voice softening. 'You never know the good you've done until years later.'

They sat for a moment in comfortable silence, letting the sounds of the town settle around them—the distant crash of the sea, the murmur of families settling in for the night, the squeal of a wagon's axle down the street.

Job tipped his beer towards William. 'To old skills—and stubborn men who refuse to drown.'

William clinked his bottle back with a grin. 'I'll drink to that.'

The conversation drifted then to the war brewing in Europe.

'You reckon we'll get dragged in if it kicks off over there?' Job asked.

William's smile faded. 'If Britain's in it, we're in it. That's how it works. Our Lads'll be signing up in droves, you watch.'

It was a Saturday morning when Ella burst through the door, eyes wide.

'Dad! What should I do , when we went to babysit for the Greaves last night he hit her. right in front of us. We couldn't stop it. She just… crumpled.'

Job sat stunned as the girls took turns recounting the scene. The bruises, the shouting, the fear.

Job, slammed his fist on the table. 'No woman deserves that.'

He said little more, but a week or so later, walking home from the docks, he spotted a figure hunched near the dunes, hidden among the saltbush crying. It was Mrs. Greaves, her face battered, her body shaking.

'Mrs. Greaves?' he said softly, crouching beside her.

She looked up with hollow eyes, she recognised Job as the father of her babysitters, the girls often telling stories of their father and how much they loved him. So he felt like an old friend and she just opened up.

'He treats me like livestock. Only kind when people are watching.'

'You can't stay there,' Job said. 'You deserve better.' But we have four sons she stammered. 'What about them?'

She clung to him, sobbing. That moment, something shifted. Compassion, loneliness, and pain swirled into something more. Over the coming weeks, they met from time with Job offering his shoulder to cry on.

When Alice discovered she was pregnant again — just as Job fell gravely ill with typhoid contracted from a recent docked ship — her body and spirit felt worn almost beyond bearing.
Job was hospitalised for weeks, his skin pale and hot with fever, his strong frame reduced to a shadow of itself.

Alice held the family together, fearing for his life, managing the household and children while carrying another child inside her.

Late one night, sitting by his bedside in the dim light of the hospital ward, she laid her hand gently over his.

'You have to fight, Job,' she whispered, her voice shaking.
'You don't get to leave me alone with all these bairns — not yet.'

Job, barely conscious, squeezed her fingers weakly.
'Not... leavin'... you,' he rasped.

She wiped her eyes quickly and forced a smile he probably didn't see.
'I'll hold you to that,' she whispered.

Horace arrived in 1905 after a long, painful birth.
When the midwife finally laid the baby in her arms, Alice looked down at the tiny, squalling bundle and shook her head in exhaustion.

'That's it,' she declared firmly to the quiet room. 'No more. I'm done.'

Later, after Job had regained enough strength to walk again, they sat together on the veranda, watching the children play.

Alice rested her head back against the chair, her voice steady but soft.

'Eight children, Job. Eight. My body can't carry another. We have to... stop.'

Job's face, leaner now after his illness, tightened briefly.
He reached across and took her hand — rough, calloused fingers enclosing hers with unexpected gentleness.

'I know, Alice,' he said, the words catching slightly in his throat.
'I'll not ask more of ye.'

They sat in silence for a long while, the easy comfort between them now tinged with something harder — something unspoken.

It was a quiet torment for Job, but he would honour her wish.
Abstinence, hard as it was, became their unspoken agreement — a silent space growing slowly, year by year, between the boy from the London streets and the woman who had crossed the world for him.

By 1909, things were looking up again.
William's building business was booming.
Both families, eager for something lasting, invested in land in Darkan — rumoured to be perfect for orchards.

One warm evening, after they signed the papers, the four of them sat under the back veranda sharing bread and cold beer, the contracts spread out on the table.

'So what'll you call yours, Job?' William asked, pouring another glass.

Job leaned back, a dry smile playing at the corners of his mouth.

'Beer Bottle Farm,' he said.

The table roared with laughter.

Alice nearly dropped her glass, giggling so hard she had to wipe her eyes.
'Only you would think of that!'

William slapped the table, still laughing.
'Typical! Trust you to name your legacy after a pint.'

Even Eleanor chuckled, shaking her head fondly.
'Just be sure you plant more peaches than beer bottles, Job.'

It was a good evening — one full of easy laughter, warm light, and hope for the future.

They cleared the land, built a rough homestead, and planted rows of young trees.
The peaches and apricots promised a golden future — until the kangaroos, heedless of all human plans, made short work of the tender saplings.

By then, Henry and Joseph were old enough to cut sleepers for the railroads, working long, hard days.
Eva found work in Collie, sending money home when she could.

Alice moved to Darkan with the younger children, making a new life in the bush, while Job remained in Bunbury to earn steady money.
The older girls — Ellen, Bessie, and Rose — stayed behind with him.

It was during those long separations, the lonely months apart, that the first real distance began to creep between Job and Alice —
and it was then that the affair with Angie Greaves blossomed.

By 1913, the fracture in Job and Alice's marriage had deepened. Typhoid had left Job physically diminished for months, and while he'd recovered in body, something in his spirit had grown restless. The long silences between them stretched further, and the gentle warmth that once passed between their eyes had faded into something more distant—polite, dutiful, but no longer tender.

Alice, after bearing eight children and suffering more challenges than any mother should, had drawn a line. When little Horace arrived in 1905 after a harrowing labour, she'd turned her face to the wall in the small back bedroom and muttered, 'That's it. I'm done. No more.'

Job had nodded, even kissed her forehead, but inside he'd felt a dull ache—not for lack of love, but for the yawning absence of closeness that once anchored their marriage. Abstinence was their only option, and while he respected her decision, it weighed on him in the quiet hours.

Now, with the farm not enough to support them Job spent more time in Bunbury, helping oversee shipments at the docks and keeping company with his older daughters— Ella, Rose, Nell, and Eva—who had taken jobs or apprenticeships in town. Alice remained on the farm in Darkan with the younger children, her hands full and her gaze turned ever inward.

It was during those stretches in Bunbury that Job and Angie grew bolder. What began in whispers and wind-swept meetings became something deeper, more consuming. Their time together, though stolen and brief, was charged with laughter, tenderness, and the kind of intimacy Job hadn't known in years. He hadn't planned it. He wasn't proud of it. But he couldn't seem to turn away either.

Eventually, he could no longer carry the weight of it alone.

One evening, seated at the kitchen table in the Bunbury house, Job called his four eldest daughters together. They sat close, tea in hand, sensing the seriousness in their father's eyes.

'I need to tell you something,' Job began, voice low. 'I'm going to leave. I'm going with Mrs. Greaves, she is leaving her useless husband'

The words hung in the air like smoke. But to Job's astonishment, it was Rose who reached out first, laying a hand gently on his arm.

'We know, Dad,' she said. 'We've known for a while.'

Ella gave a quiet nod. 'We've seen how Mum's drifted. You're not the same man when you're around her anymore. And Mrs. Greaves… she needs someone who sees her. Same as you.'

Job's throat tightened. 'I never wanted to cause harm to this family. But I can't live the rest of my life just surviving. I want to feel something again. I want joy. And she—Angie—she gives me that.'

Even quiet little Eva, barely fifteen, added, 'You've always carried us, Dad. Maybe it's time we help carry you.'

And so, a plan was hatched—wholly unconventional, yet strangely united. Angie would tell her husband she was travelling to Ballarat to visit her parents, taking only a modest valise and leaving the children with the Symonds girls for 'a week or so.'

But behind that excuse lay the truth: Job and Angie were to board the eastbound train under assumed names, bound for Queensland. There, no one would know them. There, they could begin again.

The night before they left, Job walked alone to the edge of the estuary, watching the tide slip out to sea. His heart was heavy. Alice had been his first and dearest love. She had borne his children, stood beside him in poverty and plague, shared laughter and tears. But something essential between them had weathered too far.

Sometimes, he thought, a man must choose between duty and soul. And for the first time in decades, he chose soul.

'One quiet night, with only the ticking of the old clock and the sigh of the sea beyond the cottage walls, Job and Angie sat at the rough kitchen table, the oil lamp casting long shadows.

'I've told the girls,' Job said quietly, tracing a crack in the tabletop with his thumb. 'You'll come with me. Alice will have the farm. We'll start fresh — somewhere far from here. Queensland, maybe.'

Angie sat still, her hands wrapped around a chipped mug of cold tea.
The words hung in the air between them like smoke.

'But what about my children?' she said, her voice breaking on the last word.

Job looked up, his eyes full of a sadness too old for his years.
'They'll be better off with their father and his money,' he said.
'We can't provide for them, not properly — not with the way the world is.'

Angie shook her head slowly, the knot in her throat growing tighter.

'They're babies, Job. Joseph's only six. How can I walk away?'

'You won't be walkin' away,' he said, leaning forward, voice low and urgent. 'You'll be givin' 'em a chance — a roof, food, schooling. Things we can't promise 'em out there on the road.'

Angie stared at her hands, ashamed of the part of her that longed to believe him. Her fingers trembled slightly against the mug.

She thought of her children's faces — the way Bridget clutched her skirts when frightened, the way little Joseph looked at her when he was sick, trusting her to make it better.
She thought of their father too — stern, reliable, with pockets deep enough to drown in, but hands that had long since forgotten how to be kind.

And she thought of Job — solid, steady Job, who looked at her not with obligation, but with fierce, unwavering love.
With him, she could breathe again.
With him, she could begin again.

But the cost... God, the cost.

'What kind of mother leaves her children?' she whispered to the room.

Job reached across the table and took her hand, rough fingers closing around hers.

'The kind that wants them to live better than she ever did,' he said.
'And the kind that knows sometimes... love alone isn't enough to keep 'em fed.'

The clock ticked on.

Finally, Angie closed her eyes, the tears slipping free.
'I don't know if I'm strong enough,' she said.

'You are,' Job said simply.

And though her heart ached so fiercely she thought it might shatter in her chest, she knew, deep down, that he was right.

It was late one evening when Job climbed the stone steps to the Joneses' modest weatherboard cottage near Stirling Street.
The smell of hearth smoke lingered in the air, and the sound of Eleanor humming softly drifted from the kitchen.
He paused for a long moment outside the door, the weight of what he was about to say pressing down on him like a wet wool blanket.

When he knocked, William answered with a broad grin and pulled him inside with a rough clap on the shoulder, then poured him a beer.

'Well, this is a surprise, Job. Come in, come in — Eleanor's just made a batch of barley bread. You're in luck.'

Eleanor appeared from the stove, wiping her hands on her apron. She smiled — but that sharp gaze of hers, the one Job had known since 1877 aboard *The Yeoman*, caught something in his eyes before he even opened his mouth.

'You didn't come here for bread, did you?' she said simply.

'No,' Job admitted, sinking into the familiar chair near the fire, the leather worn to the shape of old friends.
'I came here as a friend... and to ask for your understandings.'

They sat, the three of them, in the soft firelight.
The kettle hissed gently on the hob, and for a moment, none of them spoke.

Then Job drew a long, slow breath, and told them, all of it.

About Angie.
About Alice.
About the silence in the marriage that had once been so full of song.
About the older girls knowing, and the plan to leave.

About the two little ones — Horace and Queenie — who would wake one morning to find him gone, and who, he knew, would hear their mother's bitter voice spitting the words he could almost hear already:
'He ran off with that hussy. Left us to fend for ourselves.'

His voice cracked when he spoke of them.

'I ain't worried for the older girls,' he said hoarsely.
'They've seen the truth and made their peace. But the little ones... they'll hear only her anger. They'll grow up thinkin' I was the villain in a story they never asked to be part of.'

He bowed his head into his hands for a moment, the shame and sorrow rolling over him like surf.

William sat motionless, elbows on knees, his face shadowed and still.
Eleanor turned away to the window, her hands gripping the sill so tightly the knuckles whitened.

'I knew something had changed,' she said at last, her voice low and steady.
'Not just with Alice. With you.'

She turned back to him, eyes glistening but clear.

'You've always been a man of conscience, Job. Even when we were young and foolish — when I nearly ruined everything trying to free William from that damned ship — you held me steady then.'

She crossed the room, pulled a chair close, and took his calloused hand in hers.

'I'll always care for Alice. She's like a sister to me. But I have seen your despair and understand why you have made this difficult decision. Her voice broke slightly, but she steadied it.
'You never meant to wound anyone. You're not running away — you're choosing to live.'

William finally spoke, his voice gravelly from long-held emotion.

'You remember when I was chained in the hold of *The Yeoman*, Job?'
He leaned forward, elbows resting heavily on his knees.
'You said to me that night — 'There's more than one kind of prison, mate. Don't build one of your own and lock yourself in it.'

He gave a rough chuckle, but there was no humour in it.

'I never forgot that. You helped free me from a fate worse than irons. So if you're asking for my blessing — my support — I'll give it. But know this, old friend: it's not a light thing you're doing.
You'll carry it with you... always.'

'I know,' Job said quietly.

Eleanor moved to the dresser and returned with a small packet wrapped in linen. She placed it into his rough hands.

'Dried apples. For the train,' she said simply.
Then, more Softley:
'And I have a letter you'll never read — but it's for Alice. Please give it to her, in time. When she's ready.'

Job's eyes burned, but he nodded.
'I won't betray your kindness, Eleanor. And... I'll not expect forgiveness. Only understanding, where it's found.'

She squeezed his hand.

'I won't abandon her either,' she said.

The fire crackled low.
For a few moments, the years between them — the barge boy, the prisoner, the runaway girl — seemed to fall away.
Just three souls, older now, battered but still loyal to the last.

When Job left, William walked him halfway down the road.
They embraced, two old friends who had seen too much and still stood shoulder to shoulder.

As Job turned to go, the night pressing cool around them, William called after him:

'Fair winds, Job.
You've earned some peace — just be sure you honour it.'

Job raised a hand in silent farewell and walked into the darkness, the weight of love, regret, and hope woven heavily into every step.

About Angie. About Alice. About the silence in the marriage that had once been so full of song. About the girls knowing, and the plan to leave.

The train pulled away from Bunbury station with a lurch, the wheels clattering into a rhythm that seemed to echo the pounding of Job's own heart.

He sat alone by the window, his bag at his feet, the diamond pin from the Governor still tucked into his coat — a glittering reminder of a life that now seemed a lifetime away.

Outside, the night rushed past — dark shapes of gum trees and open fields flashing by like ghosts.

Job leaned his forehead against the cold glass and closed his eyes.

Behind him, he had left Alice.
He'd left Horace and Queenie, though he was not concerned about the older girls and the boys already making their way in the world.
He'd left a life stitched together from hardship, love, mistakes, and years he could never get back.

Ahead lay Angie, who had gone on ahead— and the thin thread of hope that maybe, just maybe, it wasn't too late to begin again.

But even as he pressed forwards into the dark, he knew:
Some roads, once chosen, could never be walked back.

And some parts of a man's heart — no matter how far he travelled — would always remain behind.

By 1914, they had fled to Bundaberg, Queensland — a town of sugarcane fields and heavy, humid air, a world away from the rocky coasts of Western Australia.

Job found work on the wharves, labouring in the fierce sun, while Angie kept house in a modest weatherboard cottage at the edge of town.

That winter, as war erupted across Europe, Angie gave birth to a son — a sturdy, squalling boy they named John.

The midwife wrapped the infant in a rough woollen blanket and placed him in Angie's arms, while Job stood nearby, hat clutched in his hands, his face a mixture of awe and fear.

Angie looked up at him, exhausted but smiling faintly.
'He's strong, Job. Like his father.'

Job chuckled, wiping at his eyes without shame.
'Poor lad — already stuck with my nose, too.'

Outside their small window, the world was changing faster than they could catch up.

Recruitment posters went up on every shop wall: **'To Arms, Sons of Empire!'** Patriotic songs spilled from the pubs every evening, drunk men banging tables and singing **'Rule Britannia'** until their voices cracked.

Every week, more young men — farmhands, teachers, blacksmiths — lined up at the town hall to enlist, their faces full of excitement, fear, and something else too — a hunger to prove themselves.

Job watched them one afternoon, standing outside the post office with John cradled in the crook of one arm.

Angie stepped beside him, shielding her eyes from the sun as she looked out over the crowd.

'Will it reach us here too, d'you think?' she asked quietly.

Job shifted the baby gently against his chest.

'Already has, love,' he said. 'Only difference is, we haven't felt the worst of it yet.'

Angie tucked her arm through his.

'You think they'll call for older men too?' she asked, half-joking, half-afraid.

Job gave a dry chuckle.

'I'm too old, too salty, and too much trouble for any officer to want,' he said. 'But if they get desperate enough, they'll take anyone who can still stand.'

He looked out over the swelling crowd of recruits — boys in rough boots, stiff new khaki, eager to be off before they even knew what they were heading into.

A shadow crossed his face.

'Truth is,' he muttered, mostly to himself, 'the top brass hasn't the faintest idea what's comin'. Still dreamin' of sabres rattlin' and horses charging — when the next fight will be machine guns and wire, and a man lucky to keep his head on his shoulders.'

Angie glanced up at him, hearing the bitterness in his tone.

'You really think it'll be that bad?'

Job's jaw tightened.

'Worse,' he said quietly.
'Won't be glory they find over there. It'll be mud, and blood, and boys dyin' by the thousands while some stuffed shirt back home counts the cost in neat columns.'

They stood in silence for a long moment, the weight of his words settling heavily over them.

John stirred in Job's arms, letting out a small, sleepy sigh.

Job looked down at the tiny face tucked against his chest, and his grip around the boy tightened slightly — a silent promise, fierce and unspoken.

Whatever the world became, he would do everything in his power to keep this child from being swallowed by it.

It was a grey afternoon when they posted the first casualty lists on the board outside the Bundaberg Post Office.

Word had spread quickly, and by the time Job and Angie arrived — John bundled against Angie's chest in a sling — a quiet, uneasy crowd had already gathered.

No music now.
No cheering or waving flags.
Only the shuffling of boots on dust and the low murmur of names being read aloud.

Job stood at the edge of the gathering, cap in hand, jaw set tight.
Beside him, Angie rocked gently on her heels, instinctively trying to soothe the restless baby who stirred at the tension in the air.

A young clerk stepped forward, paper trembling slightly in his hands.
He cleared his throat and began.

'Private James Arthur Bennett, killed in action at Gallipoli...'

A gasp somewhere in the crowd. A woman pressed her knuckles to her mouth.

'Corporal Thomas Henry Walsh, missing presumed dead...'

The names rolled on, steady and brutal.

Men who had been loading sugar just weeks ago.
Boys who had shouted themselves hoarse at footy matches.
Young men Job had nodded to in passing at the wharves, never guessing they'd be gone before the year was out.

Angie leaned closer.

'They're just names,' she whispered, her voice shaking.
'But it feels like losing pieces of ourselves.'

Job nodded, staring straight ahead.

'That's 'cause we are,' he said quietly.

When the list ended, no one cheered.
No one spoke.

Somewhere down the street, a church bell began to toll — slow, hollow notes drifting over the roofs of the town like a shroud.

Job pulled Angie close, resting a hand on the baby's back.
The world was bleeding, one son at a time.
And no corner of it — not even their small, sunburnt corner — would be spared.

.The weeks passed slowly in Darkan.

Alice had grown used to Job's comings and goings—he was often needed in Bunbury for long periods, where the older girls were working and the docks still called him as the sea once had. But this time was different. There were no letters. No messages. Only silence.

She busied herself on the farm, hands stained from soap and soil, days filled with keeping the younger children fed and the animals tended. But something gnawed at her—a restlessness, a knowing without proof. Her nights were haunted by dreams of trains and oceans, and she'd often wake to find her hands trembling without reason.

The girls wrote, of course. Polite letters. News of the town. But nothing of Job. Nothing direct. Just enough to keep her from asking.

It was Eva who finally broke.

One Sunday morning, after the others had gone to church, Alice was sorting linens in the back room when she heard quiet footsteps. Eva stood there, her face pale, her hands wringing the hem of her apron.

'Mum,' she said softly, 'there's something I need to tell you.'

And so the truth came—not all of it, not their role in the plan, but enough. That Job had gone. That he wasn't coming back. That he had left with Mrs. Greaves

Alice sat down, hard, on the edge of the bed. She didn't weep. Not right away. She simply stared ahead, as if trying to see something that had long since disappeared over the horizon.

'I knew,' she said finally, voice thin. 'Somewhere deep down, I knew.'

In the days that followed, the Symonds sons rallied around her. Henry and Joe had done well for themselves—timber-cutting contracts up in the Jarrah forests and a modest butcher's shop run out of the back of the old stables. They arranged for a house in town, closer to church and to neighbours. A fresh start, they said.

Alice inspected it silently, arms folded.

'It's fine,' she muttered, 'except it hasn't got a front window. Feels like a box.'

The boys exchanged glances.

That week, while she was visiting a neighbour, the lads got to work. Joe fetched his paints, and Henrey, ever the clever one with a brush, sketched a frame on the blank wall. They painted it so finely that from the street it looked like a real timber sash—complete with drawn lace curtains and a flowering geranium on the sill.

When Alice returned and saw it, she gasped.

'My Lord,' she whispered, clutching her chest. 'They put in a window.'

She stepped closer, puzzled—until her fingers met damp paint and not glass. She stared at it, then back at her boys who were trying—and failing—not to laugh.

'It's not real,' she said, voice rising.

'No,' said Henry, grinning. 'But it'll give the neighbours something to talk about.'

And it did. For weeks, townsfolk walked past and marvelled at the miracle window. Some swore they remembered hearing hammering. Others claimed to have seen a glazier's cart.

Alice, for her part, stood quietly before it each morning with her tea, watching the illusion catch the light. Something about it made her smile, though the ache inside hadn't left.

That painted window became a kind of symbol—a little piece of mischief, of beauty, of pretending things were whole even when they weren't. And in its own way, it helped.

In Darkan, life had shifted under the heavy hand of the war.
The ripple that had started in distant Europe had become a wave that reached even the most remote corners of Western Australia.

Recruitment posters appeared at the railway siding and the post office — bold, bright, and urgent: **'Your Country Needs You!'**
At first, the young men rushed to sign up — sons of farmers, blacksmiths, storekeepers — eager for adventure, for honour, for something bigger than the quiet rhythms of home.

But as the casualty lists grew longer, and the stories filtered back of Gallipoli, and France, and the endless slaughter at places called Ypres and Fromelles, the town changed.

More and more, the boys who stayed behind — needed on the farms, in the shops, in the fields — found themselves caught between shame and relief.
Every telegram that arrived was a small earthquake: sometimes delivering grief, sometimes grim silence.
And every boy left tending sheep or splitting sleepers knew, deep down, he was lucky to be alive — but would never quite say it aloud.

At the Symonds farm, the war tore its own holes.

Henry — strong, serious Henry — had signed up early, almost before Alice could blink.
Joseph, or Joe as he was always known, followed not long after, standing a little taller as he scribbled his name on the enlistment form.

Alice had tried to be brave the day they left, waving them off at the siding with a smile fixed tightly to her face.
But later, alone in the house with only the ticking clock and the whisper of the wind through the jarrah trees, she had cried — deep, silent sobs for the boys she had raised with blistered hands and aching love.

The younger son — Horace— was still too young to go, though at school the boys talked endlessly about what they would do *when it was their turn.*

Alice, watching them from the doorway one afternoon as they played at soldiers with sticks for rifles, felt her stomach twist painfully.

'You boys stay right here,' she muttered under her breath, though she knew the day would come all too soon when she could no longer keep them safe.

Even the old men in town, men who had once fought in colonial skirmishes or sailed under far flags, felt the pull and the shame.
No one was untouched.

No hearth was without its empty chair.
No heart was without its quiet fear.

.

The painted window on the little house became something of a town curiosity, and Alice found herself laughing—genuinely—when strangers would ask who installed it so quickly.

'Oh,' she'd say, lips twitching at the corners, 'it was a bit of Symonds magic.'

The farm had been handed over to the older boys, who were now running timber contracts when war broke out, supplying meat to half the district. Alice had moved into the town proper with 11-year-old Queenie and 9-year-old Horace. Her home was small but always warm, always with something on the stove. Neighbours would drop by with gossip or baked goods, and she, in turn, offered quiet wisdom and the occasional sly joke.

But the ache hadn't fully left her.

Then, one day—weeks after the truth had been revealed and accepted in painful silence—Eleanor Greaves knocked at her door.

They sat at the kitchen table as they had a hundred times before. Eleanor held something wrapped in oilskin.

'I have something,' she said softly. 'From Job. He asked me to give it to you… when I felt the time was right.'

Alice took the bundle and unwrapped it. Inside was a folded letter and, carefully tucked beside it, a pressed violet from Breaksea Island.

She didn't speak as she read. She didn't cry either. When she was finished, she laid it flat and stared at it for a long time.

'Did he ask forgiveness?' she asked, voice low.

'No,' Eleanor said. 'But he asked for understanding. And he said he never stopped being grateful for the life you built together.'

Alice nodded slowly. 'He was a good man. And I was a good wife. But sometimes two people just… reach the end of the same road.'

Alice kept her name, of course. She'd earned it. And the children would always carry the Symonds name with pride.

After a while Henry, who was home on leave offered his arm. 'You alright, Mum?'

Alice smiled. 'I'm alright. Just… a bit lighter, I think.'

That night, she sat in her little parlour, a gentle breeze stirring the lace curtains. She lit a single lamp, poured herself a cup of tea, and looked out at the painted window across from her chair.

In the quiet, she whispered, 'Goodbye, Job,' and meant it.

Meanwhile back in Bundaberg

By 1918, Bundaberg had begun to feel like home to Job and Angie.

The little cottage on Quay Street was weather-worn but filled with life. Angie kept the garden tidy, coaxing tomatoes and marigolds from the sandy soil, and Job had become a familiar figure down at the docks—gruff but fair, with stories that kept the younger deckhands hanging on his every word.

Their life wasn't without challenge. Gossip had followed them north for a time, a letter here or a word there. But Queensland was full of people with pasts—runaways, reinventions, and second chances. Soon enough, they were just another couple carving out a life.

The guns fell silent in November 1918, half a world away from the sun-bleached streets of Bundaberg and the red dirt farms of Darkan.

For days, it barely seemed real.

In Bundaberg, word spread slowly — first whispered in the cane fields, then shouted from hotel verandahs and church steps.
Bells rang out across the town, their thin, frantic peals filling the heavy tropical air.
Children danced barefoot through the streets; old men raised battered hats to the sky.

At the cottage on the edge of town, Angie stood at the gate, John clinging to her skirts, and watched as neighbours hugged, wept, and cheered.
She smiled, but it was a quiet, tired smile.
The war had taken so much — from the world, from every heart — that even in victory, the grief still lingered just beneath the surface.

Inside, Job sat at the table, a mug of black tea cooling in front of him, staring at nothing.
When Angie touched his shoulder, he blinked and gave her a small, worn smile.

'It's over,' she said softly.

He nodded, but didn't speak.
The men who had left Bundaberg's wharves at the start of the war had not all come back.
And the boys still growing — lads like little John — would grow up in a world changed forever.

In Darkan, the news arrived with the morning mail — a crumpled newspaper and a telegram tacked crookedly to the post office door.

Alice stood on the veranda of the farmhouse, shading her eyes against the glare, as Henry and Joe rode up the dusty track.

Both had survived.
Both were home.

But the war had etched itself deep into their faces — a heaviness around the eyes, a stiffness to their shoulders that no mother's embrace could ever fully erase.

They swung down from their horses, Henry with the slow, careful movements of a man who knew how easily bodies could break, Joe with a bright grin that didn't quite reach his eyes.

Alice rushed down the steps and pulled them into her arms, her heart hammering in her chest.

'My boys,' she whispered. 'My boys are home.'

Horace— still too young to have been sent to the front — hung around the older boys, listening wide-eyed to half-told stories of foreign cities, endless trenches, and friends left behind.

The Symonds sons had returned older, wiser, and changed in ways too deep for easy words.
But they had also returned determined — quietly vowing that they would live lives worthy of the mates who had not come back.

They took up their tools again, clearing land, splitting sleepers, mending fences battered by time and weather.
Henry spoke of building something permanent — a new shed, a new orchard, something rooted firmly in the good red earth.

Joe, always the dreamer, talked about travel, about one day seeing more of the world — but for now, he stayed, his hands and heart devoted to rebuilding what the war had scattered.

By the time 1919 rolled into the heat of summer, the farms around Darkan were stirring back to life.
The scars of the war ran deep, but life, stubborn and green, pushed through the cracks.

At the end of long workdays, the Symonds family would gather on the front verandah — mugs of tea, plates of barley bread, the sun bleeding out behind the hills — and they would sit together, not always speaking, but always near.

They had survived.

And they would honour the fallen, not with grand speeches or parades, but by living each ordinary day with quiet strength, steady hands, and grateful hearts.

For Job and Angie came the chance to visit Melbourne.

Eva and Eddie McDonald had written in early 1918 with news of their first child was due , and an open invitation to visit. Job hadn't seen Eva in years—not since before she'd married Eddie and moved east—and the thought of reuniting with one of his daughters stirred something deep.

It took some arranging—John was just over six years old—but by the winter of 1919, Job and Angie with John boarded a coastal steamer bound for Victoria.

Melbourne was bustling, colder than they expected, but alive with energy. A rather pregnant Eva greeted them on the platform with a tight hug and teary eyes, clearly surprised to see the lines on her father's face softened by something close to contentment.

When they reached the McDonalds' modest home in Fitzroy, Job introduced Angie and Angie introduced John .

'This,' she said softly, 'is John. Your brother.' As John went exploring as six year olds do.

Eva blinked, stunned. She hadn't expected that.

Eddie stepped forward, lifting the boy with practiced ease and giving a low whistle. 'Anither Symonds, aye? He's a bonnie wee rascal.' Said Eddie in his broad Scottish accent.

Eva was quiet, her eyes flicking between Job and Angie. 'He's beautiful,' she said at last, and meant it.

Over the next week, the visit became a gentle weaving of old and new threads. Eva watched her father with John and saw a different man than the one she'd grown up with—less hurried, more tender. Angie, though cautious at first, found warmth in Eva's kindness and Eddie's easy humour.

One evening, as the men talked over beer in the back garden, Eva and Angie sat together in the front room. Angie held John in her lap, rocking gently.

'He wasn't planned,' she said suddenly. 'But he saved us. Gave Job something to anchor him again. Gave me something to hold when I wasn't sure I had anything left.'

Eva nodded slowly. 'It's strange, isn't it? We lose so many people along the way. And then—one day—a new one arrives, and suddenly the world feels possible again.'

When they parted, Eva slipped a note into Job's coat pocket.

It read: *We all make choices, Dad. Some painful, some beautiful. This one seems to be both. I'm glad I got to meet him*

The Later Seafaring Years and Beyond

Job was a man changed from the rough-edged wharf boy he once was. He carried himself now with quiet authority and a sailor's stoic calm. Angie, ever by his side, brought warmth and laughter to the home, quickly folding herself into Eva's life as if she'd always belonged.

But Job couldn't stay landbound for long. Within weeks, he was back aboard — this time on the east coast's bustling coastal steamers. The war had ended, but the seas were still busy, and experienced hands like Job's were in demand. He crewed small freighters and mail boats up and down the shoreline, from Melbourne to Bundaberg, Sydney to Newcastle, hauling goods, livestock, timber, and stories from one port to the next.

By the mid-1920s, Job had earned a reputation. Among wharfies and shipmen, he was known simply as Captain Symonds. It was a title spoken with respect — not because he shouted or barked, but because he always knew what to do in rough seas, and he did it with grit and grace.

While others chased bigger vessels and foreign routes, Job stuck to coastal waters. He liked the rhythm of it — the way a man could pull into a familiar port, tie up, and know which tavern had the best stew and who'd still pour you a schooner with a crooked grin.

In the 1930s, as the Great Depression bit hard, shipping too felt the squeeze. Freight was leaner, and contracts less steady, but Job held his course. He often said, 'The sea's honest, even when she's angry. That's more than can be said for half the landlubbers runnin' the banks these days.'

In 1938, at the age of 70, Job finally hung up his cap.
He'd sailed long enough, seen enough, and his knees didn't like the ladders anymore.

Retirement didn't sit easily at first, but Angie, always patient, let him find his own rhythm.
And most days, Job found it at the dockside taverns — sitting in the corner with a pint of bitter, spinning yarns to anyone who'd listen.

They called him 'Cap'n' there too. Even the barkeep. Even the young ones who'd never stepped on a ship.

Job's stories were rich with salt and storm — of ships lost in fog, cargo nearly swallowed by the Bass Strait, and one tale about a wild-eyed parrot that refused to abandon ship even in dry dock.

By the time the 1950s rolled in, Job had slowed considerably. Angie's health had begun to falter in the years prior, and by 1951, she was gone — slipped quietly from his life after three decades at his side. That same year, far across the continent in Western Australia, Alice too passed on. Two women. Two chapters. One heart stretched between them.

The house in Bundaberg felt too still after that. He missed the roll of the sea, yes — but more than that, he missed the steady rhythm of Angie's voice in the kitchen, her footsteps crossing the boards. He missed Alice too, though he hadn't said her name aloud in years. It would rise in his thoughts sometimes, like a slow wave — not to haunt him, but to remind him of where it all began.

And so, in the quiet that followed, Job often found himself on the verandah — pipe in hand, gaze fixed on the horizon — letting the stories come back on the tide.

The Second Harvest

Reflecting on the Children

The light was fading.

Out beyond the river, the sky was sinking into the kind of soft purple that only came in autumn. The wind had quieted, the trees still. The only sound was the old rocking chair creaking beneath Job as it moved gently back and forth.

He sat with his pipe unlit, held loose between two fingers, the bowl cold. He didn't smoke much anymore. Just liked the feel of it — the rhythm, the memory.

'You'd have told me to light the damn thing or put it down,' he muttered with a small smile, glancing towards the empty chair beside him. 'Would've nagged me about the smell too. Every time.'

Angie had been gone a year now.

Thirty years they'd shared, give or take. Not married, not legally. That had never seemed to matter. She came into his life like a warm wind in winter — steady, sure, and full of her own fierce light.

And before her... Alice.

'My Alice. 'He whispered the name like a prayer.

He'd never divorced her. Never could. Even when the years grew cold between them, even when the distance became more than miles — she'd been his wife, the mother of his children. She was still part of him. Always would be.

Two women. Two loves. One life stretched long between them.

The rocker creaked again as he shifted.

'Nine children,' he said aloud, as if counting them one more time would keep them close. 'And not a plain one among 'em.'

They were scattered now — some near, some far. But he remembered them all as they were once: running barefoot across the paddock, laughing in the rain, curled up by the stove in winter, squabbling over nothing and everything.

He chuckled softly.

'They were different as chalk and cheese, those kids. Lord, weren't they just. Rose with her fire, Eva with her quiet heart, John always lookin' like he was off to war... and Ella Bessie, steady as sunrise.'

But what stayed with him wasn't just their differences — it was their closeness.

No matter how wild the world grew around them, Alice's children had stayed close, tethered by something stronger than blood.

'They looked out for each other,' he said. 'Still do. Alice would've been proud. Angie too.'

The pipe slipped gently from his fingers and landed in his lap. He didn't notice. His eyes were fixed on the fading horizon, lost in the gold and the shadow.

For a long while, he said nothing.

Then, almost to himself, he murmured, 'Maybe I wasn't a rich man. But I was a lucky one.'

The stars were starting to come out.
And so the old man sat, wrapped in memory, and love, and the slow breath of twilight years.

The story of Job Symonds, it seemed, was still being written — now in the lives of his children.

The chair rocked once more then stopped.

'The world hushed around him, and Job Symonds, father, sailor, dreamer — smiled. He had done his job.'

Final Chapter: The Last Wake – A Table for Job

In every family, there comes a day when the stories must be told — not for the dead, but for the living.
And in the telling, the past walks through the door again, sits at the table, and reminds us who we are, and who we came from.

It was the winter of 1956 when the letter came. It was a simple envelope from Queensland, the writing firm but slanted with age.
Inside; a short message:
Captain Job Symonds has passed. Quietly. Alone. Cairns. June 3rd.

No funeral to attend.

No final voyage to witness.

But for the eight children of Job and Alice Symonds, something deeper stirred — a need to gather, to remember, and to honour the man who had shaped their lives, each in such different ways.

So they came.

From Boddington, from Bunbury, from Perth and Melbourne — even from the far reaches of Sydney and Queensland — the sons and daughters of Job and Alice arrived in Fremantle, where it had all begun.

They met not in a grand hall, but in the upstairs room of an old weatherboard house by the sea, rented for the evening.

A fire crackled in the hearth. The table was set with mismatched china and bottles of wine opened with laughter and sighs.

Eva brought her famous scones, still warm from the train.

Joe came with a bottle of home-brewed stout.

Ella Bessie's youngest grandson helped her up the stairs, holding a dish of stew she'd insisted on bringing herself.

John, known as Jack — Job's youngest and son of Angie — stood back for a moment before entering, unsure how to bridge the gap between the siblings who had known their father best and those, like him, who had known him least.

But then someone — maybe Grace, maybe Dot — raised a glass and said simply:

'To Dad. To the Captain.'

And the room lifted in one soft, echoing voice:

'To the Captain.'

They spoke as families do — over food, through laughter, between silences.

Each memory was another candle lit in the dark.

Eva remembered how he once slipped into her wedding without a word, walking her down the aisle like a ghost made flesh.

Joe told of building fences and felling trees on land Job had claimed, and of a work ethic passed down without need for speeches.

Ella Bessie, eyes damp but smiling, recalled the letter he'd sent from Eva's house — 'Still a wild rambler,' he had called himself. But she remembered the tenderness too, folded in his words like pressed flowers.

And remember how he taught us how to sail in Bunbury , remember Nell when we both won in that regatta, yes Dad was a great sailor and he taught us well,

'Oh yes,' said Nell. What about when he had a barney with the Yacht Club president and he spat the dummy and resigned as timekeeper. He did have a temper our dad.

Then Eva piped in. 'Yes but he was also a charmer. I remember when he dropped in to see Eddie and me after Ean was born , he would play his concertina to all my girlfriends and charm the socks of them all.'

Rose, sharp as ever, leaned forwards with a sly smile.

'Do you lot remember,' she said, raising an eyebrow, 'how we four girls helped hatch the plan to let him go with Angie?'

There were a few chuckles, and some more raised eyebrows.

'We knew,' Rose continued. 'We knew the marriage with Ma was done long before anyone said it out loud. So when Dad came to us, all torn up about leaving... we told him. 'Go, If you stay, you'll only tear us all apart worse.''

Nell nodded, adding,
'We knew he'd cop it from Ma, and we knew we'd cop it too, but it was better than watching them both fade into ghosts.'

There was a long silence — respectful, reflective.

'And speaking of ghosts,' Rose grinned wickedly. 'Who remembers Rottnest? The time Dad scared the wits out of the whole school?'

There was a ripple of laughter.

'He made a pair of stilts,' she said, laughing, 'and covered himself with a white sheet. Stalked through the settlement at dusk, moaning like a lost soul. Sent the lot of us shrieking into the scrub!'

Even Joe laughed at that, nearly choking on his beer.

'And you Nell,' someone said, grinning, 'you were in the thick of the garden raids, weren't you?'

Nell nodded proudly.

'We used to pinch veg from the island gardens,' she said, 'but Dad — he'd stand watch, fiddling with his concertina. And if the guards were coming — he'd switch tunes quick as a wink and start playing 'The Campbells Are Coming'!'

The room burst into laughter.

'And we knew,' Nell said through her laughter, 'as soon as we heard that tune — drop your carrots and run like the blazes!'

Someone thumped the table in delight.
Someone else wiped at their eyes.

It was as if for a few precious hours, they were not grown children with burdens and regrets, but the wild, fearless brood Job had once loved and led — through lighthouses and storms, through hardship and laughter.

Then there was a pause — not awkward, but expectant.

All eyes shifted, gently, towards Horace.

He sat back in his chair, arms folded, gaze on his plate.
For a long moment, the only sound was the clock on the mantel.

'I was just a boy,' he said at last, his voice low. 'Nine, maybe ten. When he left.'

He looked up. His eyes were sharp, not angry, but not forgiving either.

'Ma never got over it. Said he ran off with that woman — Angie. Called her a hussy right to her last breath. And when you hear that enough... it settles in your bones. You don't ask questions. You just... believe what you're told.'

The room stayed quiet. Grace reached over and touched his wrist.

Rose said nothing, for once.

'But then I'd hear things — from you lot. Little things. Letters. Bits of stories. That he still wrote. That he asked after us. That he showed up when he could.'

He let out a long breath.

'I suppose what I'm trying to say is… I came tonight because I needed to see it. To see you. To hear him through your voices. Because I've never been sure if I was grieving a father or a stranger.'

Eva rose quietly and walked behind him, placing her hands gently on his shoulders.

'You're not alone in that, Horace. None of us got all of him.
But we all got some of him.
And maybe, just maybe, that's enough.'

Horace nodded, once.
A small tear rolled down his cheek, and he didn't wipe it away.

After Horace spoke, the room stayed quiet, heavy with old grief and new understanding.

Grace squeezed Horace's wrist.
Rose sat in silence, for once letting the weight of his words settle over them all.

But it was Queenie who broke the silence next — soft, almost hesitant.

She shifted in her chair, her hands twisting in her lap before she lifted her chin.

'I felt it too,' she said, her voice steady but low.
'The things Ma said... they were all I ever knew.'

Everyone turned towards her — the youngest daughter.

'I was so young when he left,' Queenie continued. 'I don't remember much. Just... Ma crying sometimes. Cursing his name under her breath. Telling anyone who'd listen how he'd abandoned us for that woman.'

Her hands gripped the edge of the table.

'For a long time, I hated him without even knowing why.'

Jack looked down at his hands.

Eva bit her lip.

'But then,' Queenie said, her voice softening, 'I started hearing different stories. Little things... from you all. Letters he'd sent. Money he posted when he could. How he still asked after us — after me.'

She gave a small, sad smile.

'I realised... maybe he hadn't left me. Not the way I was told. Maybe... he just couldn't stay.'

She wiped at one eye quickly, embarrassed.

'I guess I needed tonight too. To hear him properly. From those of you who really knew him.'

Joe reached across and placed his big, rough hand over hers without a word.

There was a long moment where no one spoke — not from awkwardness, but from something deeper.

A recognition that each of them had carried a different piece of the same father.

Some bright.

Some broken.

But all real.

After Queenie spoke, the fire crackled softly in the grate, filling the room with a golden hush.

Jack, standing by the hearth, cleared his throat.

'I'd like to say something too,' he said, shifting his weight awkwardly.

The others turned towards him, some nodding, some smiling encouragement.

'I didn't grow up with you lot,' Jack, now in his forties, began, his voice roughened slightly by nerves. 'I knew you existed — Ma mentioned you sometimes — but you were just... names to me. Names and faraway places.'

He paused, looking down at his boots.

'I used to wonder, as a kid, what it would've been like.
To have brothers and sisters around the table every night. To scrap and laugh and get into trouble together.
Instead, it was just me and Ma. And Job when he was home.'

He looked up, his gaze meeting theirs — strong now, steady.

'I remember meeting Eva and Eddie, and little Ean, when I was about six.
Just for a short while.

But I never forgot it — never forgot how welcome I felt. Like I belonged somewhere... even if I didn't quite understand it then.'

He swallowed, voice thickening.

'And being here tonight — hearing your stories, seeing how strong that bond is between you all — it's... well, it's made me wish I'd known you all much sooner.'

He smiled then — a small, honest smile.

'But I'm grateful.
Grateful that even now, you've made room for me.
As if there was always a place set at the table, waiting.
And I reckon Job would've been proud of that.'

He raised his glass.

'To family — the ones we knew, and the ones we finally found.'

There was a murmur of agreement, soft but strong.
Several glasses lifted in silent salute.

And for the first time, Jack truly felt it — the thing that had always seemed just out of reach.

Belonging.

And the evening continued, a little heavier now, but also more honest.

They sat for hours sharing more and more stories.

Sharing pie.

Passing bottles.

Filling the night with the sounds of remembrance.

At one point, Ean sang one of Job's old sea songs, and Dot joined in.
They were not in tune. It didn't matter.

At the end of the night, as the fire burned low and the plates sat empty, they stood together — the nine of them, and some of their families — and looked out the window towards the dark harbour.

It was there, long ago, that Job Symonds had stepped off a ship with nothing but grit and a name.
A London boy with salt in his lungs and a future to forge.

He had built a life from splinters — raised children, lost love, wandered far, and returned again in pieces.

He was flawed.
He was fierce.

He was theirs.

And now, he was home.